NEON NOTHING

RYAN MCKINNEY

From the tiny acorn...
Grows the mighty oak.

This is a work of fiction. References to real people, events, establishments, organizations, or locales are intended only to provide a sense of authenticity and are used fictitiously. All other characters, and all incidents and dialogue are drawn from the author's imagination and are not to be construed as real.

Printed in the United States of America. For information, address
Acorn Publishing, LLC, 3943 Irvine Blvd. Ste. 218, Irvine, CA 92602

www.acornpublishingllc.com

Interior designed by Kat Ross
Cover design by Damonza

ISBN-13: 979-8-88528-060-0 (hardcover)

ISBN-13: 979-8-88528-059-4 (paperback)

Library of Congress Control Number: 2023914878

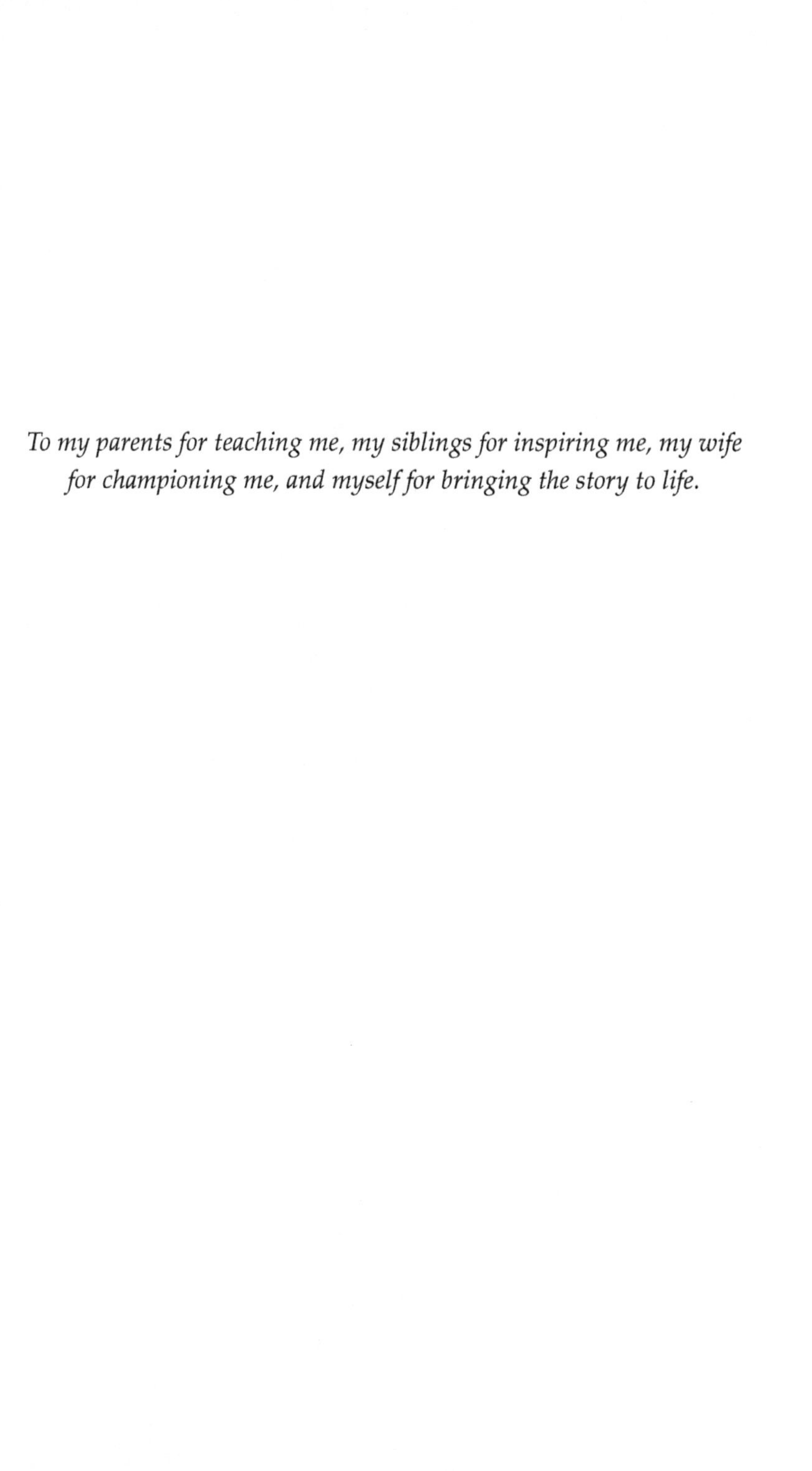

To my parents for teaching me, my siblings for inspiring me, my wife for championing me, and myself for bringing the story to life.

CONTENTS

CHAPTER 1
EMPTY

Key was a man without a past.

He barely even had a name. Sure, everyone *called* him Key, but it wasn't his name. Not really. For three years, he had tried to find the truth of who he was, but he came up empty. Still, he kept up the hunt, needing to find the truth, needing to stop his nightmares.

We're going to do wonderful things to you.

That phrase haunted his thoughts and penetrated his dreams. He napped more than slept, only getting one or two hours of sleep at a time — four at the most. He was never rested, his dreams robbing him of any repose, so he slept more. He wanted desperately to find his past, hoping that maybe, just maybe, he would finally get some peace.

We're going to do wonderful things to you.

He found himself on a table, wires and tubes coming out from all over. Some small fragment of cognition knew he was dreaming, but he was not in control.

"Bone saw."

He didn't know the voice and he couldn't see the face, the surgical light blinding him from seeing much at all. He felt the tear of flesh and the sawing of bone as the surgeon cut into his arm. He tried to scream, but there was no noise. Wires sprang from inside of his mouth, writhing like snakes. The wires grabbed his dismembered arm, drawing it into him. He swallowed it, a surge of pain emanating from his stump as it tried to grow back.

"A failure."

The voice sounded disappointed.

"We'll try again with the leg."

The saw pressed against his skin. The first bite of the teeth into flesh propelled him back to the waking world. Most people would jolt awake plastered in a cold sweat, crying out into the night.

Key didn't.

He had been through all of this before. And he knew he would go through it again, over and over, until he put the past to rest. He closed his eyes.

He was still so tired.

SUKOSHIO — "SHIO" to his friends, when he had them — was unremarkable in most ways. He looked generically "Asian," as if such monikers mattered in a post-Earth society. Neither ugly nor handsome, athletic nor fat, he had the kind of face you'd see a million times and still be able to forget. He was smart, once — gifted, even. He had earned awards in school and was showered with words like "brilliant," "genius," and "prodigy." Yet, for all his promise, nothing ever came of him. His friends got jobs and moved away, but Shio remained.

Now, six years after graduating from college, he was a customer service representative, fielding calls from clients who had purchased a Class-2 Artificial Brachius and had also purchased the limited extended support package — eat shit otherwise. When he had first begun, he tried his best to stay positive with the customers. He'd smile, even though they couldn't see him, telling himself "you can hear a smile." He'd since given up on that, and, with the increase in complaints and malfunctions, he couldn't be bothered to resume. Still, for all the mind-numbing work and failure to live up to his promise, he dreamed of something greater. They were daydreams, surely, nothing he actually intended to act upon, but he dreamed nonetheless. He knew that he had found the slot into which he fit; he wasn't getting out of it.

Bing.

A soft chime in his headset alerted him to an incoming call. Daydreaming would have to wait.

"Hello, Kigen Technologies Customer Service, how can I help you?"

He followed the script, his voice flat and empty. He'd learned it didn't matter what he said or how he said it. The people calling him were probably just going to scream profanity in his ear anyway.

"I understand," he said. "Can you elaborate on that?"

He didn't really care. It frequently occurred to him that he probably should, but that knowledge did nothing to change the fact.

"Certainly. Just let me take some notes so that we can get this taken care of."

We. As if he had any stake in it.

"Alright," he said, habitual, almost trance-like. "I have forwarded that along for you."

In truth, he didn't know if anyone ever read his notes. He wrote them dutifully and sent them where they were supposed to go, but they seemed to just vanish into the abyss that was the network. Maybe they did actually have a destination.

He imagined grabbing ahold of his notes, clutching them tightly as he rode the stream from his computer to the company's hub. Someone he had never met, likely from a different office, plucked him from the hub, opening his message to scan through its intricacies. Words like "malfunction" and "limb rejection" bolded for emphasis. He'd typed so many of these messages, and yet it only just occurred to him the gravity of having your shiny bionic arm suddenly go haywire and break all your plates. The thought amused him, though he knew it shouldn't. Satisfied, he hopped back into the hub, riding an email back to his computer.

Beep.

He was jarred from his thoughts by the gentle sound of his shift ending. It was a soft, unobtrusive sound, but it still managed to startle him.

Joylessly, he and the other fifty-nine suits stood from their desks and marched out to the hall. They waited for the elevator, silently, heads bowed as if in prayer. When the doors opened, they filed in, descending floor after floor in complete stillness. The slight *whoosh* of their vertical descent was almost like a lullaby. This was the Galivarian dream.

Galivaria: the baptized world. Though not a water world like Ys or Kitezh, it was covered in a constant deluge that enveloped it like a gray, woolen blanket. In the old world, back on Terra, before the Singularity sent humanity to the stars, there were legendary cities of industry. New York, Beijing, London, Tokyo. All were known the world over as hubs of progress, but they were supplanted by Galivaria. They say that coming to Galivaria is a chance to make a name for yourself. That the rains of this world wash away the weak, leaving only the strong behind. Maybe that was why everyone dumped their problems down the drain — but the sins had to go somewhere. They settled in some gutter or alley of her megacities. For all the massive, ad-filled, technicolor beauty that painted the nights, and the tranquil patter of the rain by day, Galivaria was far from paradise.

Most Galivarians were pencil-pushing salary workers whose only destinations in life were their cubicles, tiny one-room apartments, and eventually, the grave. What they did left no lasting mark on the world, and their names were never engraved on brass plaques under a weirdly intense portrait of themselves.

Those who did manage to get their little one-foot square of recognition still left no imprint. In ten years, no one would know anything about them. They'd have their portrait and their plaque and the gold-plated watch, but, ultimately, they were forgotten, too. The only people who had any staying power were the ones who managed to get their names on a building. The founders of Galivaria's corporations were the only ones that anyone would ever remember. Even then, only the sky would shed tears for them when they finally bit the dust.

If they bit it.

The planet's crown jewel was Hajishin Chakumari, the City of Beginnings. To those lucky enough to call the city home, the pinnacle of their labors was the one-hundred-and-eighty-story monstrosity called "Zaibatsu." Those standing at the gates of adulthood, those yet to take the test and have their fate decided, gazed at Zaibatsu in wonder. Greater-cosmic-being willing and test scores providing, each one hoped that their future would carry them to Zaibatsu. Within its walls were three of the largest companies in all of Galivaria, each holding sixty floors.

It was through Zaibatsu, her many floors rushing past, that Shio and his compatriots descended. Sitting atop the brightly-lit pillar was Kigen Technologies, their employer. If there was one company that made Galivaria spin, it was Kigen. Revolutionizing the field of biomechanics, they were the first to create a prosthetic — true prosthetic — so perfectly integrated with the body that the difference was indistinguishable. They were the first to create bionic bodies for people who had less than one-third of their body remaining. They designed augmentations for the army, making soldiers faster, stronger, and more enduring than any mere mortal.

Descending sixty floors, they passed through the Endo Printing Company. A foreign visitor might be stunned by the fact that books were still quite popular on Galivaria. It's not as though they had yet to invent a handheld device that was more than capable of containing a library's worth of literature. No, they simply liked the feel of paper between their fingers. Though they had long left the past behind, remnants lived on — a feeble attempt to kindle the "Galivarian spirit." Things like preserving the ancient palaces with parks that no one ever walked in and continuing to read paper books made them feel like the old ways were still with them. Endo Publishing certainly didn't complain. It was that very spirit that paid their salaries for the last eight-hundred years.

Occupying the bottom sixty was the illustrious Hyakuman Bank. Catering to only the richest of clients, Hyakuman was the literal foundation of Zaibatsu. Its money built the tower and its clients were the lifeblood. Simply to sit in the lobby was a gift to the senses. The entire place smelled of incense, notes of flowers and spices filling the air with a perfume that made it feel more spa than financial institution. The chairs were the finest wood and leather, each desk made from hand selected timbers. Gold and silver — the real metal, not just imitation — adorned every surface. The bases of pillars, the trim of desks, all shone with an opulence that defied logical decision-making.

The elevator denizens didn't much care for the ostentations or pompous circumstance of Zaibatsu. They had their cubicles. They had their work. Not much else mattered. Once at ground level, they all disembarked, walking in lockstep to the doors and out into the rain.

Most had umbrellas. Shio did not.

CHAPTER 2
THE WRONG SIDE

Shio couldn't decide if he was going to run or walk to the station. He had heard somewhere that you get wetter when you run. He settled into a brisk gait, the water streaming down his face, soaking his clothes, his hair, making his entire being feel heavy. It was always sprinkling, but that day it poured.

Or was it night? Honestly, you could never tell since the thick, gray clouds never let the sun through. That day, the sky was black, and the rain fell in great blobs of water. Calling them "drops" was to undersell. They were far too large for such a tiny word, and they drenched far deeper than the skin. Though he had sweltered in the humidity on his way to work, the rain now chilled him to the bone.

After a few blocks, he reached his train stop. There was a SkyBus just outside Zaibatsu, but he couldn't afford the ride. Instead, he took the commuter train, plastered in graffiti and the aftermath of the previous night's Transpo-Rave. It smelled of piss and sex, vomit and the sterile stench of drugs, but he only had to endure it for so long.

He stared out the window at the rain falling on the city. He watched the wall, plastered in stark white, that separated the Lower Third from the rest of Hajishin. On one side, respectable society. On the other, the Sundowners. In there — on the other side — in the shadow of the wall, beneath the skyscraping towers and interwoven streets — sometimes literally, oft metaphorically — the Sundowners made their lives. Unlike the rest who simply floated through life, carried by the current of routine, the Sundowners were stones, sinking to the bottom. For most, their role in society was a job. It was a self-accepted label. The Sundowners sat at the bottom of Galivaria, bathed in the metaphorical runoff of the upper echelon, so-called because, while "respectable" folk ruled the day, the night belonged to the outcast. The options were to get on board, helping minute by soul-sucking minute to press on to the brighter tomorrow all the billboards and company websites promised, or to leap off the wagon, sinking into the muck and mire of a Sundowner.

The rain never bothered them. Most spent all their time in a dark room lit only by a series of screens, each vying for their attention. Some decided to take the plunge, strapping on a Deep Dive Set and a waste bag so they could enjoy the bliss of the virtual world for a few days. There were hackers, prostitutes, drug-addled burnouts who would do *literally* anything for their next high. The Sundowners took all types. Or, rather, the Sundowner *were* all types. Whether or not they were accepted into the ranks had little to do with the will of others. Most of the time, it was a simple fall off the precipice. One step too far and you tumbled down to the bottom.

A pang of anxiety hit Shio's heart as he stared at the wall. It was an aura of dread, like being on the wrong side of the glass at the zoo.

Stay in your lane.

That's all there was to it. As long as he toed the line, did his job, maintained normality, he'd be fine. He'd stay on this side of the wall.

Half an hour later, he was exiting the train, still drenched, barely holding back the gag he had felt the entire ride. Strangely, he didn't mind the rain now. He walked a few more blocks, moving along the wall towards his apartment, running the last stretch to make it under the awning that covered the entrance. The building was old, built from brick and mortar instead of cement and glass, but he liked that. It was one of the few things he could actually say he liked.

Entering the building brought a whole other wave of sensations. Thankfully, he left the bustle behind when he left the city, but the green-tinged bulbs that lined the hallway still gave him a migraine. Up four flights of stairs, he slipped his key — a metal key — into the door and walked in.

"Hello," his apartment's AI chimed. "I'm glad you're home. How was your day?"

"Aimee" — that was what he'd named it — "shut off vocalization until morning."

He was mildly proud of the name. He'd struggled to find one with "a" and "i" in that order, though he realized later it wasn't that hard. She was helpful, automating so much of his daily life he barely had a worry in the world. She managed temperatures in the apartment, dispensed food and water for pets, and kept his schedule. Not that he had much of one to track.

He walked to the dispensary cabinet in the kitchen as Aimee pulled him a beer. He didn't even have to ask anymore. He took a swig, all but falling into the couch as he tried to sit. His dog, a twenty-pound shiba as loyal as anything with a curled tail and ginger fur, hopped up next to him and laid her head on his lap.

"Hey, Chibi," he said, absently petting her head.

He took a sip of beer, staring at the black TV screen. He could faintly see his reflection in the abyss of silent pixels, his hair matted to his head and face, and clothes wrinkled and heavy. Suddenly, he became aware once again of his wetness, taking another sip of beer before rising and heading for his room.

He stripped off his drenched suit and piled it in the plastic bin in his closet. Taking his beer with him, he stepped into the shower, a shiver almost making him spill.

"Aimee," he said, putting a hand into the water, "play Shower Mix for me."

Smooth, lo-fi synth came over the apartment speakers as Shio moved his body into the stream of water. It stung at first, hot and cold battling it out on his back as shower and rain fought for control. Soon, the shower won, filling his veins with a renewed sense of comfort. With a slight grunt that made him feel instantly older, he sat on the shower floor, letting the water cascade over him as he continued to drink.

"Just forty-two more years," he mumbled, taking a big swig, "Then I get a shiny watch."

He leaned back, face tipped towards the ceiling as the shower pelted his stomach. He drank his now warm beer, tossing the bottle into the trash when emptied. The cacophony of glass made him feel just a little self-conscious, realizing just how often he drank in the shower.

He sat there for some time, listening to the music as it lulled him into a sense of comfort and peace. This was his ritual: rise, work, drink, sleep. He used to spend time with friends, but they moved on to new phases and experiences. He checked the group chat he had with his college buddies from time to time, but he felt so alienated from them. They had kids. They had wives and careers. Shio had a dog and a bucket full of beer bottles next to the shower.

What a joke . . .

Grunting again, he rose from the floor of the tub and exited, burying his face in a towel and working it down until he was dry. Or at least as dry as he would get. One never truly gets "dry" when they get out of a shower.

Pulling a pair of boxer briefs and some sleeping pants over his still slightly damp legs, he sat at the opening of the hole in his wall — his pod — where his bed was, Chibi leaping up beside him. Again, he petted her absently. He rose to don a shirt, deciding the night was done, and crawled into the chamber, snuggling under the covers, as Chibi burrowed into the other side. He actually cracked a small smile as he looked at her innocent face, so full of vibrancy and love. He closed his weary eyes and quickly fell asleep.

CHAPTER 3
AGAIN, INTO THE RAIN

The next morning came too soon. It always did. Key felt like an undead, shuffling through the apartment as he grabbed a nutria bar and sat on his porch stoop. Jacket on, hood up, the rain barely touched him as he took absent bites of his meager breakfast.

It wasn't like he didn't have other options — his wife always kept their groceries stocked — but he didn't want to eat it. She had already left for the morning, going off to do her meaningful work as a surgeon, leaving him to fend for himself. It was never great when he did.

I should really go to the office.

He called it an office, but it wasn't much of one. It was a small room over a noodle shop a couple blocks away. He had a sign in the window of the shop and a nameplate on his door, but it was a broom closet compared to just about any office outside of the Lower Third. Well, that was life.

Should check in with Enoch, too.

There were a few things he *should* do, but he couldn't make himself do them. After the nightmare he just had, he was more desperate than ever to figure out who he was — why he was haunted by these visions of gore and butchery. He had tried and tried to solve the puzzle on his own, but he hadn't gotten much of anywhere. He didn't have a whole lot of options left.

SHIO WAS SIMILARLY unprepared for his morning, oversleeping and being in a whirlwind rush to get out the door. He always stuck to a routine, waking naturally even before his alarm, but he had slept through it that morning. He didn't have time to wonder what was off, though, as he swiped breakfast out of his kitchen, prepared not by human hands but the preset services of Aimee. He stuck half of a bagel sandwich in his mouth and gave Chibi a final pat on the head before leaving for the day.

He boarded the train, this one even worse-smelling than last night. There had definitely been a Transpo-Rave. As always, he gritted his teeth and bore the discomfort, caught between a desire to fall asleep and be freed from the torture, and to stay awake so he wouldn't miss his stop. Ultimately, the torture won, keeping him from the sweet release.

Joining the flow into the elevator, ascending the floors, and spilling into the hall, Customer Service Office Four had begun another day. In near synchronicity, the sixty suits all sat in front of their computers, put on their headsets, and waited. It never took long.

"Good morning, Kigen Technologies Customer Care, how can I be of service?"

He always started a little stronger. He was far from energetic, but he was at least more responsive.

"I'm so sorry that happened," he said, some actual inflection in his voice. "Can you give me more details for my notes?"

He typed, nodding as though that meant something.

"Absolutely."

For once, the customer wasn't yelling, just very concerned. That made his job easier.

"I have forwarded that along for you."

A couple more keyboard clicks and the call was ended. A couple more minutes and another began.

"Good morning, Kigen Technologies Customer Service, how can I be of service?"

Call after call after call, a couple minutes at a time, and he had fielded a personal record — one-hundred and thirteen by lunch.

With the soft *beep* of the overhead, it was time to eat. He went to the vending machine in the break room and ordered his usual: a turkey, bacon, ranch sandwich and a soda. He sat at his usual spot in the farthest corner. Everyone liked to sit near the door. It seemed to give them a sense that their day was moving quicker when they got out of the door sooner. He had no such predilection. He preferred the corner because no one bothered him. Not that it mattered since no one ever talked to him anyway.

Fifteen minutes later, the break ended and everyone returned to their cubicles. Seven hours later, the day was done. He wished that it was seven hours to lunch and five hours to the end of the day, but it wasn't his choice.

KEY STOOD outside the main offices of Gunto Medical and Personal Information Securities — although no one called it that. To the vast majority, they were Med-Sec; to a few they were GM Piss. Regardless of the name, Med-Sec was the premier in medical information and security. For over a century, it had been vital that extra measures were taken to ensure the confidentiality of medical records and research; these were people's lives and livelihoods on the line. That's where Med-Sec came in. In time, they went from simple file encryption to full-on secret police.

I hate this.

He couldn't suppress his dread. Still, he was left with few options. For three years, he had tried to do it on his own. It was time to enlist some outside sources. Who better but the people with a file on every person on the planet?

Nothing to it but to do it.

Key walked in the front door, the black-clad and heavily-armored jackboots reminding any and all who strode through the lobby exactly who they were dealing with. He eyed the automatic rifles strapped to their chests.

"It's cool," he quietly assured himself. "I'm just a normal citizen exercising my rights."

Though true, the facts did little to assuage the fear that gripped his heart. He held the vial of his blood a little tighter as he approached one of the clerks.

"Yes, sir," she said, looking up from her computer. "What can I do for you this evening?"

Hesitantly, Key pulled the vial of blood and his Detective badge out of his pocket. The clerk scrutinized his badge, cautiously glancing out of the corner of her eye at him. Key wasn't surprised. The Detectives of Galivaria were not like the Dick Tracys and Sherlocks of Old Terra; those were the Police Inspectors. However, those Inspectors stayed busy enough to leave some meat for the rest — meat the Detectives were ready to bite. In simple terms, Detectives were mercenaries. They had licenses to carry guns and were tried under different laws than a common civilian in the case of a violent altercation in the course of their work, leading many to be wary of them.

"Looking to get this sample analyzed?" the clerk asked.

"Yeah," Key said. "It's uh . . . it's for a case."

He wasn't quite sure why he decided to lie. He really was innocent in all of this. Still, the nightmares made him feel a certain trepidation at revealing his past to anyone. Not until he understood it himself.

"I can definitely do that for you."

The clerk opened the vial, drawing some blood into a pipette. She inserted it into a port on her Scan-r-Deck, tapping a few keys to start the analysis. Key always wanted a Scan-r-Deck, but only a few were allowed to have them. Still, they were an interesting piece of machinery. Got some skin? Scan it. Got some spit? Scan. Jizz? Scan. A single machine that could extract the DNA from a single cell — an investigator's dream if only they could get ahold of one.

Badeep.

The tone pulled the clerk's attention back to her screen. She turned pale.

Shit.

She tried to maintain her composure, but there was no hiding her immediate panic. Key could see it plainly. His hand trembled a bit, ready to pull his gun at a twitch.

Unfortunately, he'd left his weapon at home.

"Where did you say you obtained this sample?" the clerk asked, voice a little shaky.

Key saw her arm move, no doubt pressing a panic button.

"What's wrong with the sample?"

"Nothing, sir," the clerk said, eyes darting between him and a nearby guard. "If you'll just answer the question for me?"

Key heard the guard approaching. His heart jumped into his throat as he snatched back the vial and ran from the counter.

"Get that sample!" the clerk yelled.

The guard gave chase as Key ran to the door. It was locked, but it was also glass. Key punched a metal fist through it and dashed into the rainy night.

As the chime signaled the end of the workday, Shio and his compatriots rose from their desks. Again, into the elevator and down to the earth. Upon arriving in the lobby, a roll of thunder echoed through the luxury, drowning out the soft music with a guttural roar. Lightning flashed through the plate glass, turning the street to daylight — a strange sight — before rattling the glass again with thunder. No one paused, opening their umbrellas, diving into the rain, and making their way home.

He boarded the train. It smelled of lemon and rubbing alcohol.

Must be cleaning day.

His eyelids were heavy as he sat down, threatening to close for good. Every blink was harder. Finally, he lost his strength.

It was a dreamless sleep. If you'd asked him, he would have said he wasn't even sleeping, just "resting his eyes." Whatever it was, it didn't last long. He was rudely awakened by a commotion, two men shouting at each other. One wore a sharp business suit, black with an iridescent sheen like the feathers of a grackle. The other, Shio couldn't get a good look at, his hood hiding his face. Having woken up halfway through their altercation, Shio couldn't be quite sure what he was bearing witness to, but he quickly gathered that the hooded man had something the suit wanted. The pair were at the other end of the train car, wrestling over an unseen object, leaving Shio unnoticed in his seat. He decided to listen, unsure of what to do — not that he would consider himself a man of action anyway. While there may have been a time he wanted to be a cop, this was not that time. When the object in question was revealed to be a gun, the seconds seemed to slow. Shio had seen plenty of guns in movies, but never in real life. Fear gripped his heart but also a morbid curiosity.

BANG!

The gunshot echoed through the car, filling his head with static and a dull ringing. The tension of the moment shattered. He was bold enough to stand as the hooded man punched the suit, giving himself some space. As the train pulled into a station, the soft chime alerting them that it was safe to depart the car, Hood bolted off the train. Suit shouted something into his wrist — unheard, as Shio's ears were still ringing — and gave chase. Shio followed.

Even as he ran after them, his thoughts were at war. On the

one hand, his logical mind was telling him he was a fool. On the other, the dreamer within was cheering him on. Was this finally the thing that would shift his life out of the dull monotony it had become? He could call it in to the cops and be a hero! Helping to clean up crime on the streets would launch him to local fame. Hell, maybe the mayor would give him a reward for stopping the two. He might even get a date with an adoring fan.

Shio chased the suit, chased the hood, across the platform. Hood leapt over benches, threw a trashcan to the ground, and made for the stairs. Shio did his best to keep up, yanking out his phone. He dialed the emergency police line.

"What is your emergency?" the AI voice asked.

"Two men," Shio panted, "one with a gun."

There was a notable sound of alarm from the operator at the mention of "gun."

"Giving chase!" he shouted breathlessly.

"Your phone will be used as a locator," the AI announced. "Please stay in the vicinity of the altercation."

It was probably just the rush of the moment, but somehow, he managed to keep up while on the phone. Suit pursued his quarry with ease, bounding over obstacles like a trained athlete and sliding down the railing of a flight of stairs. At the bottom, Hood broke left, leaping onto the tracks and running to the platform on the other side. Suit followed without hesitation, but Shio paused. Sure, he and his friends had jumped on the tracks in middle school — adolescent dares and all that — but he wasn't a dumb kid anymore.

A quick right-left-right glance showed no trains coming. With a deep breath, he jumped from the platform.

The other two were already on the other side. Shio cautiously made his way after — too cautiously, as it turned out. Sudden headlights pierced the gloom. A hot wind lifted his sweat-soaked hair. He could feel the rails vibrating now, humming through the soles of his shoes. Adrenaline flooded his mouth, bitter and metallic. A split-second decision loomed. Retreat to safety or try to make it across the tracks? He sprinted forward as the train barreled into the station. Shio leapt up to the platform, sliding on his stomach as the cars screeched to a halt. Dashing through the open doors, the three men departed moments later.

"We've got agents all over the place!" Suit shouted. "You can outrun me, but you're not getting away with that."

"I've survived worse than you," Hood yelled back, turning and running through the sliding door to the next car.

The chase resumed, but it was much shorter lived. When they reached the back of the train, Hood was trapped with nowhere else to go.

"You've got two kilometers before my associates blow the track," Suit warned. "Barely more than a minute to have me call it off."

"You wouldn't dare!" Hood yelled. "I know he placed a call to the cops" — his extended finger pointed at Shio — "and not even you guys are that stupid."

Throughout the entire chase, neither had seemed to care that Shio was in pursuit. They hadn't acknowledged it until now. Shio wished they hadn't.

"Obviously that call was intercepted! The cops aren't coming!" Suit yelled back. "You think you're smarter than all of Med-Sec?"

Shio finally grasped the potential danger he was in. These weren't street thugs — this was an actual Med-Sec agent and his prey.

Two kilometers before they blow it.

An icicle of dread lodged in his gut. The minute was already up.

A loud *BOOM!* erupted, followed by a hideous screeching. Shio stumbled, falling into a seat as the train lurched to one side. Another piercing shriek came up from the tracks. He looked out the window, though he could already feel that the car was tilting. The train rounded a curve, giving a view of the cars ahead.

And a huge gap in the track.

He grabbed the armrest and stretched across the seats, just hoping he could hold his position. Hood and Suit were still staring each other down, neither budging as the train careened to its doom.

A wave of panicked screams came from the front of the train. Shio braced himself as best he could. Then the car shot off the shattered end of the twenty-meter-high elevated track. It seemed to fall in slow motion, the cars plummeting through the air. He drew a final gasping breath.

CRASH!

The sounds of metal crumpling and glass shattering pierced his ears. Glass exploded in a deadly rain of shards that cut his face and hands. The car behind his came down, smashing into it and starting another wave of groaning metal and whiplash. At last, after a few panicked seconds, the car came to rest.

"WH-wh-Wh-"

He couldn't think, mind clouded with fear. Shio managed to crawl out through a window, hobbling away. He'd lost his phone in the crash, but there was no way in hell he was looking for it. Besides, the suit said the call was intercepted, anyway.

The mystique of the chase gone and his own survival at the forefront of his mind, he looked around, trying to place where he was. The train had derailed near a rundown park with a few benches and shade trees, as well as a corner sushi shop. All too generic to help. The street sign read 102-12, which meant he was in Kanewara, placing him pretty far from home — way past his stop. To make matters worse, he was on the wrong side of the wall. Shio swore softly.

The Cauldron.

It was a rough part of town, so named because trouble was always brewing. Hell, the name of the district literally meant "lower living" in Common Empyrean. What was originally a geographic moniker became a self-fulfilling prophesy.

"Check for survivors!" a mechanically distorted voice called out over the crackle of the train burning and wires buzzing.

Shio thought they might be a rescue crew or the police. He broke into a shuffling jog towards the voice. As he came around the front of the wreckage, he saw six figures in black tactical gear, the blaze of the fire casting their ballistic masks in a menacing, hellish aura. Worse was the gleaming firearms in their hands.

Nope, he thought.

He broke into a sprint in the opposite direction, but the group had already taken notice.

"Pursue!" the distorted voice commanded.

Now the prey, Shio dared not turn. He had no idea what the guys on the train were doing, but it didn't matter. Those were Med-Sec jackboots if he had ever seen them, and he was not looking to get flatlined. Hood and Suit were probably dead, and he would be, too, if he didn't get away.

At least two sets of footfalls splashed through the rain behind him. After a block, they opened fire. Bullets whizzed past. Panicked, he tripped and fell into a puddle. The men in black must have thought they hit him. They stopped firing and slowly approached. Shio pretended to be dead, though his hands were shaking.

Suddenly, he spotted Hood, sneaking down the street. Shio weighed his options. Should he try to get Hood's attention? Would he even help if he *did* notice?

The men in black walked up. One of them poked him with a boot. With no other option, Shio shouted to Hood. A boot slammed into his side. He rolled to his back and saw the barrel of a gun aimed at his forehead.

BANG!

KEY HAD BEEN through some shit. He'd spent three years dipping in and out of trouble, weaving around the gutters that he and his fellow Sundowners called home. Why did he have to run? He could have just cooperated back at their office. What compelled him to pick a fight with a titan like Med-Sec?

I mean, technically, they picked the fight with me.

Didn't matter why; he did it, and this unfortunate industry drone on his shoulder got caught in it.

"Jeeves!" he yelled. "Get the door!"

"Right away, sir," a digital voice replied in a perfect mimicry of a Terran English accent.

The door slid open, giving way to Key's dark living room. Pink and green neon spilled through the far window from the corner bodega, but that was barely enough to navigate. Still, Key was able to haul the man into the room. He heaved him onto the couch and dashed off to find something to help the situation.

"Six!" he yelled. "Six, wake up!"

Unable to find any first aid, he came back with a washcloth, pressing it to the side of the guy's head. Behind him, a young woman emerged from the shadows of the bedroom.

"What's up . . .?" she asked sleepily. "Why did you —"

She stopped short, eyes wide and locked on the body.

"What the hell?"

"He got shot, Six!" Key spat. "He followed me and some jack-boots shot him."

"Move," Six ordered.

Key did as he was told. Six sat down on the coffee table, leaning over to inspect the man's head. She squinted but couldn't see anything in the dim lighting of the neon coming through the window.

"Lights, Jeeves."

"Of course, madame," the AI replied.

The lights came on, flickering for a moment before bathing the room in soft, yellow light. Six leaned in, grabbing the man's head as she examined him. He winced in pain, and even let out a whimper before Six let go of his head, turning back to her partner.

"Go to the Bug Closet," she commanded. "I need my purple bag."

Somber, Key nodded. Six looked at the man, smiling weakly.

"I'll fix you up."

CHAPTER 4
A GUY LIKE YOU IN A PLACE LIKE THIS

Shio wasn't entirely sure what happened after he took a bullet to the back of the head, but the pain of having his wound probed snapped him back to reality. He vaguely remembered the hood fighting the two men in black who had given chase, and picking him up, but he was in and out the whole time.

Now at least somewhat cognizant, he opened his eyes to see a young woman tending to him; he remembered the hood calling her Six. He looked her over, now able to see thanks to the overhead lights. She was pretty — despite having been asleep — her wavy red hair falling all about her face in a disheveled mess, but it suited her. Grabbing the band around her wrist in her teeth and pulling her hair up into a sloppy bun, Six had a face of determination. Shio found that to suit her, too.

Before Shio had time to process much else, the now de-hooded man returned.

"Purple bag."

Six took it, unzipping it and unrolling the bag, revealing a set of surgical tools. Her partner may have called her a doctor, but a moment of doubt overtook Shio.

"You sure you can perform surgery on me?"

Six chuckled.

"I did half of his surgeries," she said, gesturing to her partner.

He grinned, revealing that the first six teeth on top and bottom were metal, and rolled up his sleeves to show his prosthetic arms. It was then that Shio noticed he also had bionic eyes — the yellow iris glowing softly against the black sclera.

"Most important to this moment," Six continued, "I'm the one who fixed his head." She held up her hands. "Lady fingers are good for small work."

She let that hang for a moment as she selected her tools. Then she turned to Shio with a smile.

"Trust me?"

Somewhat reluctantly, Shio nodded. Six withdrew a pre-filled syringe, uncapping it and stabbing it into the flesh behind Shio's ear. The pain was excruciating at first, but quickly turned to blissful nothing. She turned Shio's head away from her as she began her work.

"So," she said, "what happened to you?"

"I got shot in the head," Shio replied.

"Yeah . . ." Six muttered. "Key told me."

"The bullet must have ricocheted off the plate in the back of my head and blasted out the side."

"And why do you have a plate in your head?"

"I fell as a kid and shattered the back of my skull," Shio answered. "The doctors replaced the bone with a plate and here I am."

He could feel dull sensations and hear the snipping of shears as Six cut away his skin.

"Key?" she said.

Her partner perked up.

"I also need you to grab my yellow bag."

Key nodded, going off and returning with a small yellow duffel. Six took it, pulling out a squeeze tube and bandages. She grabbed a pair of forceps and gauze, blotting as she continued to cut. When the gauze was saturated in blood, she grabbed another. As she went, she squeezed the contents of the tube — a milky-white substance — onto the wounds. She wiped with alcohol, blotted, and smeared, and in no time she was done, taking the bandages and gently wrapping Shio's head.

"There," Six said. "Told you I'd fix you up."

Shio absently touched his head as he looked over his rescuers and their home. He'd never been to the Cauldron — respectable folk had no reason to. Six looked nice enough, but Key made Shio squirm. Anyone who needed two total limb replacements, both eyes, and twelve teeth was up to something Shio didn't want to know about. Then again, he'd probably have bled out before he found "decent" folk in this part of town. Made him wonder what Six was doing here.

He'd hear chatter over lunch about people losing their jobs and being forced to move to the lower parts of the city. He heard about the types of people they'd become. Nothing good was in the Cauldron; it was nothing but drug addicts and thugs. Now, at the mercy of the Cauldron, Shio hoped all that was false.

"Sooo . . . what do I owe you?" Shio asked.

"Let's start with some information," Key said, glossing over the question as he sat next to Six on the coffee table. "Who are you?"

"Sukoshio."

"Do you have a last name?"

"Shimada."

Six cleaned up from her work, telling Jeeves to turn off the lights as she returned to bed. Now sitting in the dim, blurred neon filtering through the windows, Key's glowing eyes unsettled Shio. They seemed to burrow into him, looking right through.

"Sukoshio Shimada, age twenty-eight, working as a Customer Resource Rep for Kigen Technologies," Key said flatly. "You graduated with a 3.9 GPA from New Heibei High, going on to study Terran Literature at Owakuni Public College, graduating with a 3.2 GPA."

Shio sat in stunned silence.

"You live in the Suton area of Hajishin, alone, with an AI you've named Aimee and a Shiba Inu, Chibi, you paid a fortune for, as she is from a Terran-born mother and father," Key continued, before puzzling a moment. "You are such a fuckin' normie," he scoffed. "Why the hell's a guy like you in a place like this?"

"How did you . . .?"

"I have an internet uplink in my left eye," he said nonchalantly. "The more important question is why you decided to chase after me and the suit."

Shio couldn't quite make it out in the dark, but he'd have sworn he saw the shadow of a gun in Key's hand. He swallowed hard, the click of the gun's action telling him he was right.

"You just saved my life . . ." Shio murmured, "Are you really about to shoot me again?"

"It's possible. That depends on the information you give me."

Shio stared, fear turning his heartbeat to a sledgehammer.

"What do you have to do with this shit?" Key asked. "You're not Med-Sec, you're obviously no undercover Tac Op or something, so what the hell are you doing chasing me and the suit?"

"I don't know," Shio answered without much thought. "I just wanted to see what was going on . . ."

"Why?"

Key's grip tightened on the gun.

"I don't know!" Shio shouted.

He winced, dull pain radiating out from his wound. That certainly didn't do anything to help his head stop spinning. Blood loss, concussion, this entire situation — it was all he could do to sit upright. Far from home and at the mercy of a man with a gun, Shio's entire body was heavy as stone.

"Just rest here on the couch." Key patted the cushion next to Shio. "We can deal with all of this mess in the morning."

"Why are you guys helping me? I'm just some stranger that chased you on a train."

"I'm a quick judge of character. It's all but a necessity in my line of work."

"What work is that?"

Key smiled. "I'm a Detective."

CHAPTER 5
CLASSIFIED TO GUESTS

Shio had never had a run-in with a Detective. He knew their reputations as thrill seekers and money grubbers, looking to make a quick gil off of the lost and the desperate or mop up the scraps of the Inspectors. Some were able to rise above it, though, and become respectable investigators.

Key was clearly not one of them.

"Okay, Detective," Shio started, a hint of fear in his voice, "you know *all* about me, but I don't know a thing about you. I'm pretty sure 'Key' isn't even your name."

"It's my name as far as I'm concerned."

"And Six?"

He ignored the question. "Go ahead and sleep. You're going to need it."

Shio arched a brow. "You're just going to trust a stranger?"

"Hell, no," Key shot back. "Make one move — a gesture — I don't like and I will make sure you never eat soup unassisted." He held out a blanket, smirking. "But I know you're harmless."

Shio nodded, stunned. He took the blanket and lay down on his non-injured side, facing away from the glow of the neon outside.

What have I stumbled into? he thought — and fell dead asleep.

Come morning, Shio's head was throbbing. With both shock and anesthesia worn off, he felt every ounce of the pain that comes from getting shot in the head. Desperate for relief, half wanting to see what he looked like, Shio got up, sluggishly moving towards what he assumed was the bathroom. He was correct, the lights flicking on upon entry. Tub and shower combo, toilet, and sink. The room was tiled up to chest-height with earth tones and painted white from there to the ceiling. He tried the mirror to see if it was a medicine cabinet but no luck. He remembered the apartment AI.

"Jeeves?"

"Yes, sir?" the voice replied.

"Where do they keep the pain meds?"

"I'm sorry, sir," Jeeves replied, "but the location of the madame's medications is classified to guests."

"Where are the bandages?"

"I'm sorry, sir, but the location of the madame's bandages is classified to guests."

"What about . . . the meds from last night?"

"I'm sorry, sir, but the location of biohazardous waste is classified to guests."

Smart. Living in a place like the Cauldron, it's no wonder she's careful.

He dared not wake Six or Key — definitely not after what Key said the night prior — nor did he want to go outside the apartment. Just then, Six walked past the bathroom. Shio stepped into the hall, noticing that Six had prosthetics herself; it was just visible from the hem of her shorts, but, from the mid-thigh down, both her legs were inorganic.

"Six," he called after her, "where are the pain meds?"

She turned to him, walking over to the bathroom. "Well,

aren't you presumptuous. You already owe us a mountain for saving your ass last night. You want to go ahead and add 'demanding house guest' to your bill?"

Shio shook his head.

"Have a seat." She pointed to the toilet.

She left, briefly, returning with another syringe like the one from last night. She carefully unbandaged his head, revealing the wound beneath.

"Can I see it?" Shio asked.

Six nodded, chuckling. "If you think you can handle it."

He walked to the bathroom mirror. The side of his head was shaved and his skin flecked with dried blood. The wound was massive, stretching from just behind his ear to the back of his head, all the skin flayed off, revealing the metal plate beneath. Shio felt sick, stumbling back to the toilet to sit.

"I thought it might be a little much to look at," Six said.

"Did you . . ." Shio paused, breathing deeply to quell the nausea, "did you *have* to skin me alive?"

"Yes, actually." Six looked mildly annoyed by someone questioning her methodology. "The bullet must have fragmented *bad,* because most of the skin was already separated from the plate, and the surface looked like cartoon cheese."

"Half the skin on the side of your head was shredded by what I can only assume was shrapnel, and you were bleeding profusely," she explained. "So, yes, I had to cut it all off and clean the edges so you wouldn't get an infection."

Shio felt guilty for doubting her. "You're like . . . a real surgeon."

"I'm not 'like' a real surgeon," Six spat. "I *am* a real surgeon."

Shio felt even more guilty. He was also realizing her chipper bedside manner had worn off.

"Is it —" Shio stopped, not wishing to dig the hole even deeper. "Is it normal for Sundowners to have so many bionics?"

"What do you mean?" Her voice was still a little heated.

"I mean Key has both arms, his eyes, and part of his skull —"

"He's got a lot of cyberware," Six interrupted. "What's your point?"

He thought on that a moment before continuing.

"And you have both your legs replaced. Is that . . . normal?"

Six leaned back against the sink, crossing her arms as her face twisted in thought. She gazed at the floor, then her toes, wiggling them.

"I'm normal. It's far from uncommon for us low-folk to lose a limb or two to accidents, disease, or birth defects, or to sell them to the Bio-Chic fabricators so they can turn them into their high dollar 'organically sourced' prosthetics. It's good money if you're willing to make the sacrifice."

"But Key —"

"He's special. Me and my crew found him in a bio-dump, still alive, with half his body missing."

Six fell silent a moment.

"His face was caved in and bloody, arms torn off at the shoulder, one leg broken, the other sheared at the knee . . ." She trailed off. "I still wasn't a master surgeon then, but I helped put him back together and get him back on his feet."

"Do you know what happened to him?"

She frowned. "Forgive me for being skeptical of you asking all these questions."

Shio was a little offended. A Sundowner being skeptical of him just rubbed him wrong.

"I'm just trying to understand what I've ended up in. With this head wound, I'm more or less at your mercy."

"Fine," Six said with a heavy exhale. "No, we don't know what happened or why. Only clue was a cybernetic spine he'd been implanted with, but the thing was an impenetrably encrypted mess, so all we could do was get it to integrate with his new bionics."

"It was encrypted?" Shio's face scrunched with confusion. "What does that even mean?"

Six sighed. "Every piece of cyberware — all prosthetics — have programming, right?"

Shio nodded as she spoke.

"Normally, that's a pretty easy set of files to read and understand so that there's less chance for problems and they put your patient data in there so the docs can just pull up your file, right?"

Shio nodded again.

"Key's spine had a half-dozen layers of cryptographic coding keeping anyone from reading or altering it, meaning we couldn't get much of any information on the people who gave him the implant or access any patient data that might have been in there. That's actually why Key went to Med-Sec last night; he wanted to see if they had his DNA sequence on file."

"So, he broke in?"

Six's expression soured. "No!" she spat. "He walked in the front door and asked."

"Then why . . .?"

"Must be something to do with whoever did that to him. We don't know who it was, but that kind of stuff doesn't just *happen*, and, when it does, you're sure not going to find the evidence in a bio-dump. You're chopping them up to dissolve that shit in acid."

The two sat in silence a moment, Shio processing everything he'd just been told. He wasn't sure exactly who these two were or what they were up to; he was certain he'd end up paying some kind of price for the mess he'd walked into. But he also felt like he could trust them. They'd saved his life, after all.

"I have one more question."

"Go for it," Six said, her voice a little exasperated.

She opened a small panel behind the sink and pulled out a toothbrush. She stuck it in a small hole, pulling it out with teal paste, and started brushing her teeth. Shio sat and watched, a little bit of fear showing on his face. Six glanced at him.

"Whaf da quefshion?" she asked, her mouth full of foam and a toothbrush.

"Where do you guys get the bionics?" he asked. "Sundowners are poor, so how do you afford the prosthetics?"

Six spat, cupping water into her mouth and spitting again. She rinsed her toothbrush, placing it back in the compartment, and dried her face with a small towel. It became evident to Shio that she was drawing this out on purpose.

"First of all," she said, "Sundowner and poor are not synonymous."

Shio felt another wave of guilt coming.

"We're Sundowners because we don't buy into the corporate bullshit this city — this *planet* — runs on, and don't really want to change that," Six said. "Yeah, that usually means we end up poor, because it's hard to get a job when you don't have Praedus Test scores to tell all the big men in suits how great you are, but we work hard and we make our livings."

"I —"

"As for your actual question," Six continued, blowing past Shio's interjection, "you'd be shocked what gets thrown away on your side of the wall. We don't have to buy or even steal in order to get our hands on these things" — she tapped her leg — "people just throw them out when Kigen, Nu U, or Tango-Tec comes out with the latest and greatest. It's like Minister Xiao Dewang said, 'everything trickles down eventually'."

CHAPTER 6
BRING TWO GUNS

Once Key got up, the three sat down for breakfast. Key wasn't sure what to do about this rando that had landed in his life, but he decided to give the guy a chance. If someone hadn't given him one, who knows where he'd be. Probably dead.

"You guys are married?" Shio asked.

Key hadn't caught the context for the question — too focused on making his breakfast — but his attention was certainly grabbed.

"We are," Six answered, nodding.

Shio took a sip of tea. "Weird," he muttered.

Really, Shio had a point. Marriage was considered an antiquated tradition in the Empyrean Union, but that didn't stop the two of them from tying the knot. The truth was they made each other happy, and they wanted to keep making each other happy. There was certainly nothing saying they had to, but there was also nothing saying they couldn't.

"I guess," Six replied. "It's just something we decided to do."

"And you guys are totally monogamous?"

"Pretty much," Key answered, bristling slightly. He didn't particularly like how open they were being with a complete stranger. Shio didn't need to know all of this stuff about them, he had no *right* to know all of it.

Key brought his food to the table as silence fell, the others clearly sensing Key's discomfort.

"So . . ." Shio started, trying to change the subject. "What's the next step?"

"Next step?" Key asked, taking a bite of omurice. "What are you talking about?"

"What's next?" Shio repeated. "Are we going to go hunt down the guys that shot at us or what?"

"*I* am," Key replied, mouth half full. "*You* are going to get your normie ass back on your side of the wall and forget any of this ever happened."

"How can I do that?" Shio asked, a bit incensed. "Med-Sec shot me in the head! How am I just going to pretend that didn't happen!?"

"He's got a —"

"I know he has a point," Key spat, cutting Six off.

There was a heavy silence as both Six and Shio stared at Key. He took a couple more bites of omurice.

"How about this," he said. "We take you back to your apartment — make sure everything is cool and you're safe and whatever, and *then* you go back to being a normie."

"You have to make *sure* I'm safe," Shio said. "Certain."

"Okay, okay," Key assured him. "We will." He took another bite of omurice. "But first, tell us your version of what happened last night." — another bite — "I have assumed, thus far, that you actually had nothing to do with this in first place, but you seem awful paranoid for someone who is as innocent as you let on. If people are going to be shooting at us, I'd like to know before I stick my neck out for you."

"I'm not sure," Shio admitted, looking a little dejected. "I was asleep, then I woke up and you were fighting with the suit, so I followed you." He scoffed. "Thought I might be a hero or something."

"So, why did they shoot you?" Key asked. "Med-Sec doesn't just put people down for nothing."

"Because I called out to you, Mister Detective!" Shio shouted, growing frustrated. "Why do these guys want you, anyway!? Are you some fucking lowlife with a bounty or something?"

Key stayed silent, offended by Shio's assertion.

"I'm sorry. I . . . I didn't mean that."

"You did, though," Key chided. "Just remember that you *chose* to follow after me."

"I'm just — I'm overwhelmed," Shio said. "Yesterday I was just a normal, miserable guy, and . . . now I'm not. Now I'm sitting in your kitchen with half my head flayed. I don't know what I was thinking, trying to be some big shot, but it got *me* shot."

"And I dragged you out of there."

"You're right," Shio admitted. "So, what? Can I go home, now? You guys are going to escort me? It's the least you could do for dragging me into this."

Key and Six looked at each other and chuckled. Key shook his head, face changing on a dime, going stone cold.

"I'm not going to say it again," he growled.

Key may have only been holding a butter knife, but Shio had little doubt it would be deadly in Key's hands. The fact that it was pointed at him didn't help.

"*You* followed *me*," Key said through clenched teeth. "Pin that shit on me again, and I'll make sure Med-Sec knows you're not actually dead."

The color drained from Shio's face. Key tossed down his silverware and got up from the table, heading towards his and Six's room.

"I'll need some clothes," Shio said.

"That was the plan, squib," Key called back.

"Oh!" Six called, "Love?"

"Yeah?"

"Make sure to bring *two* guns."

. . .

THE THREE RODE in the car in silence, the sounds of the road soothing what could otherwise have been a very tense half hour. Shio looked out the window at the SkyBuses and LevCars floating overhead. The only time he'd ever ridden in one was when he dated the daughter of a Tango-Tec executive. It seemed only a fortunate few got to enjoy the sky.

Key slumped in the backseat, eyes closed and arms crossed on his chest. He looked quite peaceful — possibly asleep. Shio wouldn't have blamed him. The patter of rain on the old steel roof of the car made quite the soothing soundscape. It was no wonder they called it a "Galivarian Lullaby." Shio would probably have fallen asleep himself if he weren't so intimidated.

"Sooo . . ." he said, feeling awkward.

Six cocked an eyebrow.

"I don't like prolonged silences that much," he said. "Tell me more about you guys?"

"Like what?" Six asked.

"Well, for starters, how did a Sundowner become a surgeon?"

"You're backwards."

"What?"

"I said you're backwards," Six repeated, "It's not 'how did a Sundowner become a surgeon?', it's 'how did a surgeon become a Sundowner?', and it's two of them."

"I assume it was your parents?" Shio asked cautiously.

"Yeah." Her voice was soft. "The two of them and my uncle, Doc, were surgeons way back."

"What happened?"

"The system happened," Six spat. "It's illegal on Galivaria to perform surgery on the uninsured, but they did it because they saw people lose an arm to the factory or a leg to disease and couldn't do any less than help them be whole again."

There was a heavy pause that Shio dared not interrupt.

"Shortly before I was born, the cops found out, and all three of them were stripped of their licenses, jobs, and homes, leaving them as Sundowners. When I was born without my legs, they decided to break the law, again, and fix me. Then they thought, 'why not keep breaking the law?' and opened a black-market clinic."

"They're the ones who taught you to do surgery?"

"Yep," Six answered. "But they're gone now."

The mood got heavier.

"How did — how did your parents die?"

"Mom got stabbed by a junkie who wanted some painkillers, and Dad was shot by the cops when they raided our first clinic." Six seemed shockingly nonchalant. "But Doc and I rebuilt."

A sickly feeling washed over Shio. His stomach churned, and he felt a little woozy. Was this normal!? Getting stabbed by junkies, shot by the police? Hell, they hadn't even addressed the fact that Key walked away from a train crash! Shio was just an ordinary guy. He wasn't trying to get all tied up in this sort of seedy behavior — he didn't want to *die*. He had just managed to escape! He looked out the window, hoping to get relief watching the world pass by, but that only made it worse. Thankfully, they were very near to his apartment.

"Right over there," Shio instructed, pointing to his brick-and-mortar building.

Six pulled up to the curb, throwing the car in park. A deep, awkward silence fell as the engine sounds faded, replaced only by the patter of rain on the roof. It was a pleasant sound but not enough to distract Shio from the massive slice of humble pie he was going to have to eat.

"I want to start by saying I'm sorry."

"For what?" Six asked. "For being a prejudiced dick even after we saved your life?"

"Hey!" Shio protested, "I was —"

"You were," Key affirmed, not opening his eyes and clearly not actually asleep. "I mean . . . it's fine. We'll still help you 'cause we're cool like that, but you're totally being a condescending ass."

Shio fumed. He was trying to apologize and they wanted to insult him!? His desire to make amends faded as he threw the door open and stepped into the wet. He was used to it, never having an umbrella, but that didn't stop him from being deeply cold. He stormed up to the front door, the familiar green flicker of the entryway welcoming him home.

This feels like a bad idea. Leading strangers to my house.

But it was too late for thoughts like that. Six and Key had come into the foyer behind him.

"Wow," Key said. "Been a long time since I've seen a building this old."

Ignoring him, Shio walked up the stairs. He went to unlock his front door when he realized it was already slightly ajar. Aimee's voice drifted through the crack, speaking to someone inside.

"Sirs, I really must insist that you wait for Mr. Shimada to come home."

Whoever she was talking to, they weren't heeding her.

"I can prepare a snack while you wait," Aimee continued.

For a moment, Shio regretted not getting a defense package for Aimee. Then his thoughts were swallowed as terror set in. He backed away, instinctively hiding behind Key and Six, deferring to their ability to keep him safe. Cautiously, Key drew both of his guns, handing one to Six, as he approached the door. He placed his ear next to the crack.

"I hear someone," he whispered, listening intently. "Make that three."

Springing into action, Key kicked the door open. He dashed across the small hallway on his left to take cover in Shio's combination living room and kitchenette. Automatic rifle fire erupted from the intruders, the crack and blast of shots deafening in the small apartment. After a few seconds of sustained fire, they stopped.

"Did you get a look at him?" one of them asked, voice distorted by a mechanical filter.

"No," said a second.

"Think it was the tenant?" the third asked. "This Shimada guy?"

"No way," the second replied, scoffing. "Masatori shot him — blew the side of his head out."

The three started to walk towards Key from their position in the bedroom. Shio went from terror to pure panic, hyperventilating as he backed against the wall opposite his door. Six sidestepped to the right of the threshold, gun at the ready. The three men came into view, their familiar black gear sending a bolt of lightning through Shio's spine. The fear built in seconds, erupting from Shio's mouth in a piercing scream.

"AAAAAAAAAAGHGH!!" he shrieked.

The guys in black whirled, dead-eyed masks locked on Shio. With no time to think, he dropped to the floor. Six popped around the corner, shooting one in the head, as another shot came from Key. Only one target fell. The man shot by Six staggered but was still alive — a tell-tale mark on his mask revealing the lack of penetration. Wasting no time, he charged out. Six took another shot that ricocheted off the mask. He tackled Six, knocking her to the ground. Her gun clattered down the stairs as he readied his weapon. In a fluid motion, Six kicked up, knocking the gun skyward and bending the barrel with the force.

Meanwhile, the other assailant rounded the corner to the living room, only to get knocked over the coffee table. He aimed and fired, but the bullets failed to penetrate Key's extended hand. With one hand over the nose of the rifle, fist clenched, Key struck with the other to break the front half of the barrel off. Not missing a beat, the man in black drew a knife, swiping at Key as he kicked him back, scurrying to his feet. Key still had his gun and emptied the magazine. Some bullets bounced off the mask, others struck the chest, but none felled the man in black. Out of ammo, Key raised his fists.

Six was in a similar boat, though with another wrinkle: Shio. Her adversary disarmed, he tried to leap atop Six, but she wasn't having it. She placed a hefty, metal-bending kick to the man's chest. He dropped to one knee to catch his breath. Possibly wanting to help, potentially just losing his mind from fear, Shio went wild, running at the man. The trained fighter was more than prepared, drawing his knife and stabbing it into Shio's side. Now on her feet, Six landed a roundhouse kick to the assailant's head, caving it in and partially knocking it from his shoulders.

With no one to distract his opponent, and a less advantageous venue, Key had yet to settle his fight. It became evident that he was up against the leader of the three, as he wasn't going down like a bitch. Still, it was easy enough to just use his knife-proof arms to block his body, though the ferocity of the strikes kept him on the defensive. Then a well-timed kick with his strong leg caved the man's knee to the side. He was crippled, but refused to go down, still striking at Key with the knife. The advantage now claimed, Key grabbed his enemy's wrist, crushing it in his hand. With a swift strike to the mask, he went down, Key squatting in front of him.

"Who is Sukoshio Shimada to you?" he asked, reloading his pistol. "I thought you guys wanted *me*."

The man removed his mask, gasping and panting from pain.

"As it turns out . . . he's no one," the man spat, the tiniest hint of a rueful laugh in his voice. "He just has extremely bad luck."

"Bad luck!?" Shio demanded, hobbling into his apartment.

As soon as he cleared the threshold, Aimee shot into emergency mode.

"Operator vitals are outside of acceptable parameters," she announced. "Heart rate is highly elevated and blood pressure is dropping."

"Shut up," Key spat.

Aimee ignored him.

"Calling emergency services."

"Nope!" Key shot to his feet. He dashed over to Aimee's

control panel as Shio took his place standing over the intruder. He was closely followed by Six, looking deeply concerned, as he clenched his side and winced; he was incensed, and no knife in his side was going to keep him quiet. He wanted answers.

"What the hell do you mean, 'bad luck', you jackboot fuck!?" he yelled. "Why are you ransacking my apartment!? I didn't do shit!"

"Not my job," the man groaned. "I wasn't even there for the train crash — just supposed to search your place for damning evidence. I guess we got the wrong guy, though . . ."

"Evidence of what?" Key asked, trying his damnedest to multitask as Aimee protested. "I don't even know why you guys were after me, let alone him."

The man took a swipe with his knife but missed, instead getting a kick from Six. Face plus bionic limb equaled undoubtedly shattered bones, blood pouring out of the man's nose and from his lips.

There was a burst of audio static and Aimee fell silent. Key came to join the others, wires in hand.

"I asked you a question," Key growled. "What evidence were you looking for?"

The man said nothing. Key pressed on his shattered leg, eliciting a howl of pain.

"It's not about some little salary slave," the man gasped. "This is big shit — top of the food chain shit."

"I'm not in the mood for a manifesto," Key grumbled.

"You were just an accident." The man laughed and looked at Shio. "You've just got the shit luck of being too curious for your own good. You should have never swum out of your lane, little fish. You should have stayed a boring, lifeless, hopeless fucking slave."

Shio breathed heavily, neck flushed with anger.

"I bet no one would have even missed you," the man taunted, another laugh waiting behind his biting words. "We killed the only thing that loved you."

The silence suddenly set in. Shio heard no barking.

"Chibi!"

Shio flew into a rage, pulling the knife from his side and plunging it into the throat of the man in black. Panting, he gritted his teeth as he pushed it in to the hilt. The man's labored breaths turned to gurgling and stopped.

"Damn it!" Key yelled. "He clearly knew something!"

He started to pace. Shio actually saw a tear fall from Key's cheek.

"He knew something about me," Key said, voice quivering. "I was *so* close to an answer — *an* answer."

Shio's breath got shaky. He was losing a lot of blood. Not to mention the fact that he had just killed a man. He looked into the cold, empty eyes of his first life taken. He felt sick, shock and blood loss taking hold. He vomited, then gagged again.

"I —"

He didn't finish, passing out in his living room.

CHAPTER 7
LEARNING THE DIFFERENCE

Shio came to. His eyes fluttered open as his head resumed spinning. He wanted to sit up, but he knew it'd be a mistake. The room was dimly lit, so he couldn't see much, but he could smell. The air was smoky, and he could catch liquor in the air.

He realized he must be at a bar or something, as there was a table to his left and he was lying on a booth. He decided to tempt fate and sit up. Excruciating pain shot through his side.

"Damn."

He had hoped that waking up on a bar seat meant he had simply been dreaming. The pain in his side confirmed he had not. The shot to the head, his criminal companions, his dog dying, all of it was real and ongoing. Shio heard voices. They were faint, but he recognized Six and Key; the third was foreign. He rose, shakily, taking labored steps towards the voices. He walked down a hallway lit in neon, proceeding to a *very* green door. He decided to eavesdrop.

"What do you know about it?"

That was Key's voice.

"I'm spittin', but you're not catchin', squib!"

The second was a male voice, a bit deeper and rougher than

Key's. Shio wanted to figure out who this guy was. He debated busting into the room, listening more, or just running out of the joint, never to speak of this mess again. His indecision led to him just standing there, inadvertently making his choice.

"Enoch."

Six was chiming in now.

"I handed you the goose, *kazo*," the stranger, Enoch, protested. "You wanna keep chasin' that's on you, but I told you I don't know anything."

There was a heavy pause. Shio couldn't see, but he wagered Key was staring daggers into Enoch.

"I'm not gonna look up deets on the *gasayaro* what shot at you," Enoch said. "Tha's bad karma an' I ain't messin' with it."

"Oh-ho-ho," Key chuckled. "No, it isn't."

"Whatcha spittin'?" Enoch asked, a bit incensed.

"You still owe us for that job last month," Key said. "Bad karma is turning us away."

"I paid that debt, *kazo!*" Enoch exclaimed. "Fixin' the *shironai* healin' up in my bar squared us!"

"A few staples and a quick transfusion do not cover us getting caught with two crates of bionic weapon systems by Tango-Tec and shooting our way out," Six retorted.

"You're lucky we didn't end Shifter for the bad intel," Key said.

"Not my fault you two are botchie-*baka*," Enoch said. "I just move the pieces into place. If those pieces fuck up, that's not my bag to hold."

"Look," Key said, his voice exasperated. "We're friends, Enoch."

"You're always makin' me think twice about it, but yeah," Enoch replied, "we're blood."

"Then just do us this solid," Key said. "Please."

They paused. Too afraid now to move and get a better vantage point, Shio was still unable to see what was happening in the room. He grew worried. Hang around much longer and he might get caught.

"Why this?" Enoch asked. "I owed you months back, so why you wanting to cash in now?"

"I just . . . I've got a feeling that this is bigger than a train crash and some rando."

"That's the problem, *kazo*," Enoch said. "I *know* it's bigger — fuckin' massive."

"Then why won't you help us?" Six asked.

"Cuz I'm not about to throw away my two *okini* for sometin' we got no business in," Enoch replied, suddenly solemn. "I look into this, and I'm sendin' you into the mouth of a dragon."

Fear set in, causing Shio's nausea to return. He didn't know what Six and Key wanted, but he could bet a hefty sum it wasn't anything good.

"Please," Key pled, "I didn't kick death in the balls just to hide from him."

"The danger I put you through on the regs isn't enough?"

Enoch said it like it was a joke — a rough one, but a joke — but Six and Key weren't laughing. Shio got doubly worried. Facing down the tac-team hadn't shaken them but something was.

"*Daijo*," Enoch said, giving in. "Hand em over, and . . . Imma see what I find."

Shio heard heavy thuds. He peeked around the door, catching a glimpse of Six sitting in a black leather chair and a man with pink hair sitting behind a desk. Shio had always been told not to judge birds by their feathers, but he had to admit that Enoch looked intimidating. He had brown skin — something that must have been natural given the general lack of sunlight on Galivaria — and glowing orange eyes. His arms, or at least what Shio could see of them, were gold and black prosthetics. He was also heavily pierced with studs in his bottom lip, eyebrow and ears, and rings in his upper ear and nose. Piercings in general tended to mark Galivarians as rough-folk — tattoos, too — but that many was usually cause to steer clear.

"Ey, *shironai!*" Enoch exclaimed, "Stop lurkin' and get in 'ere."

Reluctantly, Shio obeyed. He must have been spotted when he peeked in the door. Stepping in, he got a better view of things. Enoch, Six, and Key all sat in leather chairs, a large desk between Enoch and the rest. The room was evidently an office — albeit a dimly lit one — surmised from the three computers and stack of papers. What caught Shio's attention was the bionics on the desk. In three clear plastic bags sat a heart, hand, and jaw, some amount of blood and flesh still on them.

"Whatcha hear, *shiro nana?*"

Shio got frustrated. "Why do you keep calling me that?"

"Cause squib like you don't come around these parts," Enoch replied. "You keep your nose squeakin' clean — keep it white."

Anger welled up. The last day festered like acid in his chest. What the hell had he done to deserve this? All he ever did was go to work and stay home; now he was on the run from god-knew-who wanting to kill him for god-knew-why. His dog was dead, half his scalp was gone, and, worst of all, he was getting dragged around the city by the kind of sick fucks who would rip out someone's organs as evidence. Shio snapped back to his apartment. He felt the life fading from the man in black as he gripped the knife in his hand. He hadn't even felt the pain when he pulled it out to stab the man. First, he chased strangers, now he'd killed a man . . . what was happening to him . . .?

My nose isn't white now . . .

Pain swelled in his side, causing him to wince and clutch it.

"You good, squib?" Enoch asked.

"Yeah," Shio answered, voice shakier than he'd have liked. "I guess I owe you thanks for fixing me up."

"Don't worry," Enoch said. "I'll add it to your tab."

"I imagine you heard through the door," Key started, clearly a little upset at the eavesdropping, "but I guess introductions are in order."

He gestured to Enoch. "He and Six go way back, and he was one of the main guys that helped me out when I first . . . became me, I guess."

"He's been a pain in my ass ever since," Enoch added, laughing. "Wish I never knew this *baka yaro* . . . fuckin *doji*."

"Enoch," Six said, resuming the introductions. "This is Sukoshio."

"Ha-HA!" Enoch exclaimed, as if having a realization. "We're like *shinzoku, ne?*"

"What do you mean?" Shio asked.

"My *mei* — my real name — is Shirosaki," Enoch answered. "Like yours, just jumbled up."

Shio thought a moment. Why *didn't* the others have Galivarian names? Enoch did but chose not to use it. Why? Names were a big deal to the Galivarians. Unlike Terrans, Martians, Europans — anyone from Sol, really — who cared little, donning and doffing names like so many hats, to a Galivarian, a name was everything. To not only shun their family names, but their given names, too . . . what did that mean?

"What's your real name, then, Six?" Shio asked.

Six turned in her chair to face Shio. She smirked. "Earn the right to know."

Shio fumed, though he tried not to let it show.

Rude! he thought. *When asked your name you're supposed to give it!*

"Things 're different in the gutter, squib," Enoch said. "Or did you forget where you are?"

It seemed Shio wasn't hiding his emotions well. Come to think of it, he hadn't really had to. He'd been so numbed out the last few years — couldn't even remember the last time he was feeling passionate, actually — that masking emotions wasn't much of a concern. For the first time, he asked himself why that was.

He'd had everything he needed. He was raised by loving and encouraging parents, was smart, talented, and well-liked, yet he still ended up an empty, lonely shell. Why?

"I didn't forget," Shio replied, "just learning the difference."

"Well, Imma need you to learn a little quicker," Enoch said. "We about to crack a dam, an' I need you ready to swim the flood."

"What?" Shio asked, stunned. "You want me to be a part of the investigation?"

"Consider it you owing me for killing the witness," Key said. "Plus, you're the one that complicated this mess in the first place. Did you think we *wouldn't* make you a part of the plan?"

"I just . . . I'm not a Sundowner."

"You are now," Six said. "We aren't sure why these guys are after Key, but they're after you, now, too. You're burned regardless."

"Burned . . .?" Shio repeated.

"They know where you live; they know your face, and they're Med-Sec, so they know every nuance of your life," Key said. "Despite how much I'd love to just get you out of my hair, you can't go back to your life. You *have* no life anymore."

"You're a Sundowner," Six said, actual empathy in her voice.

"You can embrace it or not," Enoch said, "but, at least until we get this shit sorted, that's life."

The reality finally set in. Something clicked in Shio's mind. It was true; he'd been so furious with Key for "dragging him into it," but it was his choice. The moment he got out of that train — the moment he chose not to run the hell away — his life was over. He couldn't go back to Kigen or his home; everything in his life was gone. He scoffed at himself. The truth had been there all day, but he refused to see it. He wasn't sure what flipped the switch for him, but it was flipped. Even if only slight, a change had begun. He understood why the Sundowners took new names.

"Not much I can do about it," Shio said. "No point in fighting it."

He was struck with acceptance. Perhaps it was simply that he had nothing left to lose, or maybe it was a sudden acknowledgement of circumstance. Whatever it was, he felt it deep within himself, rising to take over his whole being. It was probably the same thing that compelled him to give chase. He could feel his face twisting in all manner of thoughtful expressions as he tried to find the way to fit this into himself — the grander puzzle that made him up. Or was he even that puzzle anymore? Sukoshio Shimada wouldn't have killed a man.

"Shio?" Six prompted, concerned.

"I don't think so," Shio murmured, half to himself. "Like Key said . . . I don't have a life anymore."

CHAPTER 8
REBORN SUNDOWNER

Shio stood frozen in Enoch's office as past and present swirled in his head. He wasn't even sure it was accurate to call himself "Shio" anymore. It was like the others said: he could never go back to his life as it was before.

He was a Sundowner. He was burned. He had taken a man's life. Everything he had built up to that point crumbled away. Perhaps it was time he learned what that meant.

"What do you mean *you don't think so?*" Six asked.

"I don't think I can call myself Sukoshio Shimada any longer . . ." Shio said, still distant. "I think whoever that was died when they shot me in the head . . . maybe in the crash."

It was a lot to come to grips with, and he felt a little melodramatic musing on his own death. Still, he was too lost in his thoughts to stop the words coming from his mouth.

"Maybe I died when they stabbed me outside my apartment," he continued. "Whenever it was, I don't think I am who I used to be. Shio died and someone else got up."

"Alright," Key said, a little amused but nonetheless engaged. "I can't say I was any less dramatic when I woke up like this."

"If not Shio, then who?" Six asked. "What's this 'reborn Sundowner' named?"

Shio thought a moment. It wasn't a deep thought — he seemed incapable of much more than superficial functioning — but he thought all the same. Only one name seemed right.

"Chibi."

Key burst out laughing. Enoch was more composed, but he chuckled, too. Six glared at both of them, turning to Shio — now Chibi — with a smile.

"It's a great name," she said. "That was your dog, right?"

Chibi nodded.

"She was a girl . . . and a dog." His eyes glazed as he stared off into nowhere. "But I feel like carrying her name is like carrying her. I didn't have much, but . . . I had her."

"Alright, Chibi," Key said, stifling more laughter. "Welcome to Sundown."

After finishing his mental processing, Chibi was taken to the bar's dressing room to get some non-knifed, non-bloodied clothes. It was his second set of ruined clothes in as many days, and it was starting to get annoying. Still, being alive and naked was better than clothed and dead. Thankfully, he wouldn't be lacking for long, courtesy of Enoch.

"Take a look, *inu*," Enoch said.

Shio was a little surprised, not just by the fact that the bar had a dressing room, but also by how nice it was. The lockers were all sleek steel designs, and the closet was a revolving wheel filled with clothes nicer than what Chibi had in his apartment.

"Bar's closed until 15:00," Enoch said. "So, you won' have to worry about anyone interruptin' you."

Chibi looked over his options, flipping through garments like files in a drawer. He was taken aback. There were silk shirts, satin blazers, ties, hats, and shoes of varied styles and materials. All the outfits were in garment bags with a picture and a list of what was contained within. Someone must have curated all the outfits. It was so unlike the varying shades of gray Shio had always worn that Chibi wasn't sure what to choose.

"I'll give you a sec," Enoch said, heading back down the stairs to his office.

Chibi continued to look through the wardrobe selection until he was struck by a particular outfit: a purple blazer and blue shirt with a pair of white pants — chartreuse pocket square and socks serving as loud accents. He'd never worn anything like it before, but it spoke to him. He felt like that was what this man-reborn should wear.

Have to look the part.

He glanced over his shoulder, making sure that no one was coming in behind him before changing. He hoped no one would walk in. In truth, he was a bit shy about whether or not he'd look ridiculous. He felt a bit like a pigeon trying to dress as a peacock.

Once dressed, he stepped over to the mirror. The various tools and palettes of makeup on the vanity suggested one of two things: this was a co-ed locker room or Enoch employed femboys. Possibly both. It was probably both.

Damn.

The last time Chibi looked in the mirror he nearly puked, the sight of his metallic skull and flayed scalp sending his head spinning. This time, he stared with cold acceptance. He turned his head to get a good look at Six's work. He had to admit she'd done an incredible job. The edges of his wound were clean, and the wound itself curved in an almost artistic way. Actually, Chibi *had* seen people get a plate grafted on their head for purely aesthetic reasons. He'd always steered clear of those types when he saw them on the train, but now who was he to judge?

This is Chibi, he thought, reaching for a pair of trimmers.

He proceeded to buzz the sides of his head, leaving a droopy mop on top. He wanted it off his face, grabbing a tin labelled "Sculpted Locks" and smearing the contents in his hair. He hadn't worn hair gel since his rebellious stage at fourteen; Chibi actually felt nostalgic for a moment. Granted, what he had back then didn't turn his hair white. Though accidental, Chibi looked himself over and decided he actually liked it.

Maybe I'll dye it . . .

He stepped back, taking it all in. Purple, blue, white, pops of vibrant green — it was more color than he'd worn in years, yet somehow it felt like a return to form. It was like he'd simply been on hiatus for a while, and now was coming back to himself.

"Shi — Chibi," Key called. "Six and I are chasing down a possible lead, you wanna come?"

Chibi smiled. He struck a quick pose in the mirror, his smile widening to a grin.

"I'll pass," he said. "I think I'm gonna have Enoch show me around."

CHIBI CAME DOWN the stairs before Key and Six departed. They sat at the bar with Enoch, discussing something Chibi couldn't hear. As he entered the room, they all turned to him.

"I like the new look," Key remarked. "Really screams 'I like selling drugs.'"

Six jabbed him with her elbow, almost knocking him off his stool.

"You really do look good," she said. "It's nice to see you embracing things a little."

"It's okay, Six," Chibi said, chuckling weakly. "I can take a joke."

A quiet settled over them as Chibi's emotions swirled. Everything was still so fresh he couldn't settle on a thought or feeling. He'd barely processed the death of his sole loved one, nor had he had time to absorb the fact that every item he owned and luxury he enjoyed was lost, but he also couldn't help the excitement at all the new in his life.

"Well," Enoch said, bringing his hands together with a clap.

"Since you are dressed, and these two have some investigation to do, I'd say it's time to start that tour you wanted."

THE TWO LEFT THE BAR. Outside, Chibi saw a sign, finally learning the name: *Kanpai*. It was at the end of an alley, flanked on the right by a placed called Lolly's — what Enoch said was a brothel-ish escort service-ish establishment — and on the left by a bank of sorts, run by a loan shark named Jimin. Whether night or thick clouds were to blame, the sky was quite dark, causing all three establishments to have their neon on, painting the alley in a technicolor glow.

Though the alley was an assault on the senses, Chibi was woefully unprepared for what awaited on the main street. They could hear the people before he even emerged, the full scope hitting when they did. A bright blue, personified bowl of ramen beckoned the two to eat him, as a pink anime girl invited them into her store. Shopkeepers stood on the streets and had booths on the sidewalk. Despite the rain, the streets were bustling — a far cry from the quick in-and-out of the uptown streets Chibi was accustomed to. He liked it, actually. There was an energy here that lifted him out of his head. It had been a long time since he had reason to pay attention to the world around him. People in brightly colored ponchos walked all over, as no cars drove down the street, the road blocked off to form the plaza. Enoch glanced over, Chibi catching it out of the corner of his eye.

"You wanna do some *kaimono, inu?*" Enoch asked. "Maybe get some *shoku*?"

"Can you . . . not use Gali?" Chibi asked.

Enoch cocked an eyebrow, half inquisitive, half knowingly accusatory.

"I don't understand it."

"You best learn, *shironai*," Enoch said, almost reprimanding.

"This place only gets busier at night, and I promise you're gonna want to catch what people be spittin'."

After an awkward silence — a bit of a guilty one on Chibi's part — Enoch relented. Still, he rolled his eyes. "Do you want to do some shopping, dog? Maybe get some food?"

"Yes," Chibi said sheepishly.

"Good," Enoch replied. "I'm starving."

CHAPTER 9
A TRAIL TO FOLLOW

Six and Key sat in the lobby of the 30th Ward Patrol Office. Any ward after the teens wasn't exactly known for their top-of-the-line offices, but the thirties might as well have not existed. The 30th looked like a rundown floor of a municipal building despite being the headquarters for an entire eight-hundred square kilometers of Hajishin.

The bulbs were dim and gave a sickly-pale light. The tiles of the floor were synthetic and chipping — something that took the better part of a decade given the material's toughness. The chairs looked and felt like something out of the twenty-fourth century, all of the padding in the seats long gone flat. Even among the wards of Kanewara — the low district — it seemed they were the bottom of the list.

I hate this, Key thought.

His legs bounced uncontrollably. A nervous tick, but odd that he had it even with his bionic leg. Usually things like that didn't carry over.

"It's okay," Six said.

She placed her hand on his thigh. His legs stopped. A feeling of peace washed over Key. Despite the circumstances and his surroundings, there was always Six to cut through it all. She kept him grounded.

"Key."

An officer came out from behind the clerk's desk, beckoning Key over. Normally, this wouldn't phase him at all; he came to the Patrol Office all the time for intel and leads when he was doing Detective work. Now, though — after the two run-ins with Med-Sec — he was wary of anyone with a badge. A police sergeant was no exception.

"You said you had something for me?" Key asked, walking over.

"Yeah," the sergeant said, nodding and speaking in a hushed voice. "But we're not going to talk about it out here."

Key was led to the sergeant's office, the door closing behind him. After a second or so in the dark, the lights flickered to life. Even the motion sensors were busted.

"So, what's the lead?" Key asked, impatience starting to take over.

The sergeant gave no answer as he walked around his desk and sat in his chair. The chair creaked and groaned as he leaned back, folding his hands on his chest.

"I heard someone matching your description broke into Med-Sec," the sergeant said, voice low but audible. "That you?"

"I didn't break in," Key corrected. "I walked in like any citizen has the right to do."

"I bet."

"Can we get to the point, Rin?" Key asked. "I know damn well you didn't call me over here to talk about whether or not I broke into Med-Sec. I told you that they were after me just by asking for info on their movements and chatter."

"You poked a dragon, Key," Rin answered. "I need to know that my sister is safe with you."

Key's mood turned.

"You make sergeant and suddenly you're worried about us?"

he asked accusingly. "Where was this concern when the cops were trying to raid the clinic?"

Key stared as Rin sat in silence.

"How about when Tengu sent the Fifth Sector into the 30th to firebomb Kanpai?"

Still, Rin remained silent.

"Just because you don't wear the angel anymore doesn't mean you suddenly have the moral high ground. That badge doesn't erase Riser the Gangster."

"I did what I did as a foolish young man," Rin said. "I walked away from that life, but I never stopped caring for you lot. Six, especially."

"Fine," Key sighed. "I don't have the energy to argue with you."

"For once."

The two men stared at each other, Key's eyes ablaze and Rin's a cold glare. Normally, Key might have punched him. It would hardly be the first time he and his brother-in-law had fought, but he thought it a mistake to do again. Not only for Six's sake, but the fact that he was standing opposite a commanding officer surrounded by his subordinates. The door might be closed, but an office full of cops wasn't something he wanted to deal with.

"Just tell me what I want to know and I'll leave you alone," Key said.

The hint of a grin tugged at the corners of Rin's mouth. He so rarely won their arguments.

"Med-Sec is being abnormally reticent," Rin said.

"Meaning?"

"You recall that I said they reported someone 'matching your description' as having broken in?"

Key nodded.

"You and I both know that they are 100 percent aware of who you are — they're Med-Sec, they know the name of every man, woman, child, and other on this planet."

Key nodded again.

"So why aren't they reporting you by name?"

"I don't know," Key said, a bit exasperated, "are you going to tell me?"

"I certainly don't know," Rin answered. "But it's odd."

"Fucking hell, Rin . . ." Key flopped into one of the chairs opposite the desk. "Tell me you didn't drag me over here for a 'hm, isn't that odd'."

"You're a Detective," Rin said. "I thought for sure —"

"Do you want to get dragged across your desk? Is that what you want? You want to piss me off?"

"Okay, okay," Rin capitulated. "I've had my fun with you."

Key took a breath. Rin was an asshole, but that wasn't reason to get himself arrested. Definitely not right now. Too much risk. Some other time, though . . . maybe.

"Med-Sec is clearly worried about you," Rin continued. "They are reporting your 'break-in' to the police out of legal obligation, but they also aren't revealing your identity with any specificity."

Key's wheels spun as he placed each piece of the puzzle into its proper place.

"They even reported the train crash in the 26th before they cleaned it up, even though they have legal protection from collateral damage when in pursuit of a target. It's not like they have reason to report it."

"So, who are they hiding this from?" Key asked. "They're a titan and I'm a peon, there's no way they're scared of me."

"Just because they're not scared of *Key* doesn't mean they're not scared of *you*."

The realization hit Key like a bolt of lightning.

"Me," he said. "They're after the old me."

Rin nodded. "I have no idea who that is, but there's no explanation I can think of besides that," he said. "It looks like you finally found a trail to follow."

CHIBI SAT in a darkened restaurant with Enoch, the glow of Enoch's eyes unnerving him slightly. It wasn't noticeable in a well-lit room, but the lights provided more glow than illumination, allowing Enoch's eyes to cut through the dim. Paired with the fact that his pink hair was nearly luminescent — there must have been a blacklight among the bulbs — and Enoch's face seemed to fade into the dark, leaving only his hair and eyes glowing in the void. Truly unnerving.

"Whatcha thinkin', *inu?* What's catchin' your eye?" Enoch asked. "I'm in here *itsumene* — all the time — so I already know what's up."

Chibi looked at the menu, graciously placed on a digital screen in the table. He scrolled through it, not answering Enoch, as he tried to figure out what to eat. It was hard to focus on the menu with the waitresses walking around. It wasn't so much them as the way they were dressed. Some of them had cat ears and cute dresses, while others wore the equivalent of lingerie. Chibi had heard about restaurants like this — eateries staffed entirely by cute girls in costumes — but had never been to one. They weren't exactly considered "societally appropriate" by most.

"*Konbanwa,* gentlemen."

Chibi was startled from his intense focus on the menu by their waitress arriving at the table. She was one of the cuter ones Chibi had seen, wearing a cupcake skirt and waistcoat.

"*Moshi,*" Enoch replied, holding out his hand.

The waitress took it, receiving a kiss. She giggled and playfully snatched her hand away.

"You're too much, E," she said, grinning. "You want your usual?"

Enoch smiled. "You got me on a string."

"And for you?" the waitress asked, turning her attention to Chibi.

Chibi froze. He opened his mouth after a second but nothing came out.

"He'll take the same," Enoch chimed in.

The waitress nodded, walking away from the table. After a moment of silence, Chibi looked at Enoch.

"Is she your girlfriend or something?" he asked.

"Or something," Enoch replied. "You gotta loosen up, *inu*," he said, changing the subject, "You gon' *sagaru* wit' us, you needa chill a bit — get *samui*."

"What does '*sagaru* wit' you' entail, exactly?" Chibi asked, half unclear what it meant and half concerned about the answer.

He hoped to get more details out of Enoch than the other two. He definitely understood why they'd be reticent to share, but it had finally clicked that this was life. Now more than ever he understood he was playing catch-up in the world of Sundowners.

"I'll spit the deets later. *Tabun*."

"I don't want to wait for later," Chibi insisted. "This is my life *now*. I have a right to know what I'm getting into."

Enoch's eyes kindled a certain spark. He kept his everyone's-best-friend smile, but there was a warning in his expression, too. Chibi was starting to realize that questioning his newfound friends was not something they liked. For once, he decided not to back down.

"Look," Chibi started, "I get that I'm the odd-man-out trying to muscle my way into your little group, but I'm here. I'm not going anywhere because I have nowhere else to go. I wouldn't dare betray you guys because I don't even know if the law would hear me out before they shot me or turned me over to the private sector, so you really have nothing to lose."

He paused his rant to give Enoch air in which to spit out a reply. Instead, he seemed stunned by Chibi's boldness.

"Do you really want to be hauling my clueless ass around Hajishin?"

"*Bangō*," Enoch admitted, holding his hands up in a tiny

gesture of forfeit. "We're a hundred times more likely to get some *gasayaro* tryin'a light our asses up for some botchie-*baka* stunt you pull because you got no marbles in that head."

"So, spit."

CHAPTER 10
STAY IN YOUR LANE

Chibi grew more comfortable with each passing song that played overhead. He could see why Enoch liked it here. Not only were the girls cute, but the music was excellent and the place had an intoxicating aroma that Chibi could only liken to the incense-filled lobby of Hyakuman. He'd never gotten the chance to linger there, but it always soothed him for the minute or two he'd get to spend waiting for the elevator every morning.

Just another thing I lost.

At least now he knew where to get his fix for pleasant aromas.

"Tell me more about yourself," Chibi said, trying to better settle in and relax — make small talk.

"Nope."

Chibi was stunned for a moment. He sipped his water.

"You already know all you need to know about me for now," Enoch said. "You know I keep Kanpai. You know I'm blooded *kazo* with Key and Six. You know this place, and you even know my *mei*."

There was a break as both men waited for the other to speak.

"You gotta start learnin' *inu,*" Enoch continued. "Sundowners don' do *chotto hanashi* like normies."

"What do you mean?"

"*Chotto hanashi* — small talk, *inu,* the little stuff that —"

"No, no, I got that," Chibi interrupted, "I mean how are the fundamentals of who you are and what you do *not* small talk?"

"It's not fundamental to us, *inu,*" Enoch explained. "Names don' mean much when you can have three or four people know you by, so we hand out that info fo' free."

"Why not the other stuff?"

"You never know who knows who knows who," Enoch said. "You let slip to some *gasayaro* that your brother is on-world for business with a client. 'Who does he work for?' they'll ask. You tell 'em he's an exec with Nu U. Some chickens talk to some foxes and all of a sudden you're getting your ass beat in a dark room while they have your brother on holo because you just became leverage in a corporate cock-block."

"Sounds paranoid," Chibi scoffed. "How the hell do you guys live like that? Never able to trust anyone?"

"We just have to figure out who we can trust. The yes and the no," Enoch replied. "Shit, *inu,* take two looks at what we're actually saying; we're calling small talk 'the chat of the deadly flower'. It's nice and all that — smells like roses — but it's just as likely to get you killed."

"I guess I just don't get it," Chibi said, leaning forward as he shook his head. "I lived the corporate life for years and I never ran into this type of stuff. People made small talk over lunch all the time, talked about their relationships and their kids, all of that."

"Uh huh . . .?" Enoch said, beckoning Chibi to continue.

"If you guys are scared of jackboots rolling up, why didn't I have to deal with the same stuff?"

Enoch shrugged. "Could be a dozen reasons. Maybe it's because the *kaiju*-corp already had their hooks in you, so they didn't have to sweat learning any dirty deets. They already knew everything there was to know about you, so why worry about hiding your *dinkei* from them?"

"I guess, but —"

"*Jigoku*, maybe it's 'cause the only time normies give half a *kuso* about us is when they want to use us for something," Enoch interrupted. "If we keep it in, no one knows anything and nobody catches bullets."

Chibi absorbed all that Enoch had explained. It made sense, it was just hard to wrap his mind around it fully. Had his life really been so different?

"We find our people — find our *kazo* — and things are cool," Enoch said. "We don't much like change."

"Is that why Key is always so uptight?" Chibi asked. "Six seems a lot more forthcoming."

"That's Six," Enoch replied. "She's the only reason that *baka yaro* isn't jus some lump o' meat in a bio-dump. We was gonna leave his ass to die. *Kanashi omae* — poor bastard, but what could we do?"

Chibi imagined where he'd be if Key hadn't saved him that night, a bullet through him, face down in a gutter. For all the complaining and generally spoiled behavior on his part, he couldn't deny that he owed Key his life and a little extra.

"Six wasn't havin any o' that," Enoch continued. "We was *gonna* save his life."

"She's not normal, then?" Chibi asked. "Altruism isn't the expectation?"

"You tell me, *inu*," Enoch said, leaning forward. "What's the unspoken motto of this world?"

Stay in your lane.

Chibi knew it all too well, but movies, TV, books, all the great stories he knew didn't fit that narrative. For the first time, the irony hit him. He had always loved stories of the self-sacrificial hero but had lived the opposite. Everyone did.

Stay in your lane.

It was the unwritten rule. Everyone on Galivaria knew that.

Whatever was happening, it didn't concern you. Stay in your lane. Beggar on the street? Stay in your lane. Guy robbing the store? Stay in your lane. It's not your problem. Don't get tied up in other people's business. The rule went so deep, some people got offended when another person tried to help without being asked. If you aren't invited, you have no place in it. Stay. In. Your. Lane.

"Exactly."

Chibi must not have been hiding his expression well, as he didn't even have to give a reply for Enoch to know what he was thinking.

"Six isn't abnormal, she's downright strange."

"I'm glad she is," Chibi said, absently rubbing his wound. "I owe everything to that strangeness."

Their waitress approached the table, breaking the seriousness of the conversation. She chatted with Enoch, but Chibi was only half paying attention. Instead, he was lost in thought, daydreaming like he was back at his desk. He imagined himself standing on the wall between the Lower Third and the rest of Hajishin Chakumari. He stared at the upper districts, dotted with lights, progress, and promise, the wall whitewashed and clean. He thought about how it had felt, once, to look at the wall and think about what would happen if he ended up on the wrong side of it. Now that it was a reality, he wasn't certain what he had always been afraid of.

"*Shironai.*"

Chibi was shaken from his thoughts. He looked across the table. The waitress was sitting in Enoch's lap.

"It's time to go check on Kanpai," Enoch said. "We've been open for an hour."

Chibi nodded.

"As of right now, *inu*, you're on the clock."

CHAPTER 11
GAUCHE TO BE MACHINE

Key's legs were back to bouncing. He sipped on his drink, trying to calm his nerves, but nothing neon purple was going to calm anything.

Think.

He tried to will answers into existence, knowing full well they wouldn't come. Still, he struggled in his mind to make something out of what little he had. At least he had something new to add to the mix. Whoever he was before he became Key, that man was someone to fear. Kind of made him feel good.

Just because they're not scared of Key doesn't mean they're not scared of you.

He thought back on what Rin had said. He tried to think of enemies of Med-Sec but knew that wasn't going to yield anything. Anyone high-profile enough for him to know by name was far from a viable candidate for his old self. They may have been a private company, but they were the unofficial arm of the Insured Medical Services Act, so it's not like the government was going to be any help. He flicked on his uplink, staring into cyberspace as searches scrolled past his view.

Med-Sec Reveals New DNA Sequencing System

Nope.

Med-Sec and Tango-Tec: A Match Made in Hell?

Definitely not.

Med-Sec to be Sued for Sequencing Individuals Without Notice

Maybe?

He searched and scrolled, searched and scrolled, all at the speed of his own thoughts. When he first got the uplink, it gave him a headache, but he'd had plenty of time to adjust. The hard part wasn't navigation anymore, it was blocking out the distraction. When your every idle thought had the potential to start you down a rabbit hole, focusing on the world got a little more difficult.

Damn it.

He blinked away the never-ending waves of the web, returning to reality. Now he stared at the far wall of Enoch's office, slumped in one of the black leather chairs. He sat up, looking at his hands. They weren't high-end, but he had smooth articulation. Unlike the now-common prosthetics that were just a robotic skeleton with silicone rubber flesh, he had actual synthetic muscles that flexed, the metallic plates shifting as he moved. It was a recent trend to shun metal, leading to a wave of prosthetics trickling their way down. For most, the new goal was to reveal as little as possible that was inhuman. That was what Kigen had pioneered, and Nu U had perfected, going as far as to use real flesh puppeted by a robotic skeleton. It was now gauche to be machine. Maybe that was why the Sundowners embraced it so hard. They *wanted* to flaunt their machine parts. They'd rip the flesh off discarded limbs so they could build it back in metal and carbon. Granted, there were those outside the Sundowner that liked the look, too. Fashion prosthetics had begun to catch on, but they were for the young and rebellious — the playboys with diamonds in their knuckles and bachelorettes with stilettos built into their feet.

How did I even lose my arms . . .?

Key never knew. According to Six, they were gone when she found him. All he'd ever known was the cold, metal hands. Artificial nerves had gone a long way, but they were still only imitations — haptics reaching for flesh and blood. The result was dull and imperfect; he'd never truly know what it felt like to hold his wife's hand. He'd never have the all-too-human moment of burning his fingers on toast or feeling them go numb from making a snowball without gloves. He certainly didn't mind the strength boost — the might to bend steel was nothing to sneeze at — but there were still things he missed. Or perhaps "missed" was the wrong word. It's difficult to miss something you don't remember.

Knock Knock.

Key rose from his chair, taking the knocks as his cue to leave. A slender woman with bright blue hair opened the door. Upon seeing Key, she held up her hand, halting him. He sat down again, as she strode over to Enoch's desk, taking a seat on it and crossing her legs.

"What is it, Nat?" he asked.

The woman tucked her hair behind her ear. "Straight to work, then." She smirked. "Where's the foreplay?"

"I'm not really in the mood."

"Awww . . . not even for me?" Nat asked, moving to the arm of Key's chair. "How about a little pleasure before business? It's been a while, but I remember what makes you tick."

Her fingers danced on his chest as she leaned over on his shoulder.

"Is this what you came in here for?" Key asked. "Because I'd wager there's a job for me."

"There is," she replied, all but whispering. "Some business with the Wires or something."

Nat wrapped her arms around Key's neck.

"If it's business with the Wires, I should probably get the deets and head out, yeah?" Key said, staying focused on the matter at hand. "Those guys are pretty impatient."

"I think some chrome-domes can wait," Nat said, nipping at Key's ear.

"Then call me overly professional," Key said, unwavering.

"Fine." Nat rolled her eyes and went back to the desk. "You and Six are so boring."

Key gave her a blank stare.

"The garage on 118," Nat said. "Twenty-three block. I think it's called Supe Ups?"

"I know the one," Key said.

"It's a routine pickup. Grab-and-go."

"Anyone coming with?"

"What do you think?"

ENOCH AND CHIBI strode into Kanpai. Open, the bar looked far different than it had when Chibi first woke up in one of its booths. Dimly lit had turned to candy-colored neon and a spinning ball that cast it all in fractal patterns of light. Empty had turned to a bustling bar filled with all manner of people. It had been a *long* time since Chibi had felt this much energy in a room. The music thumped and the lights pulsed to the beat. Chibi stood there stiffly, feeling out of his element.

"*Inu!*" Enoch shouted over the music.

He grabbed Chibi by the back of the neck, pulling him close. He got right next to Chibi's ear, speaking a bit quieter than before.

"As of now, you're my *hosa-kan* — my personal assistant," he said. "You go where I go, do what I do, and don't do what I don't. *Daijo?*"

Chibi was stunned.

"I . . . I —" he stammered. "I'm honored."

"Don't be," Enoch said, releasing his hold. "Means you ain' got trust!"

Quickly humbled, Chibi followed Enoch, worming their way through the crowd. He spotted Key doing the same in the opposite direction. Chibi wanted to get his attention, but decided against it, fearing he might lose Enoch in the throng. They made their way back to Enoch's office, closing the door behind them to seal away the party outside.

"*Suwaru*," Enoch directed, pointing at a chair.

Chibi was confused by the woman sitting on Enoch's desk, but he seemed unfazed. Chibi complied, sitting opposite Enoch. He sat awkwardly as he waited for Enoch to give another direction. He cast glances at the woman on the desk and she did the same in turn. Both seemed to be sizing the other up, though Chibi certainly knew who would be the better judge. He had learned quickly that the Sundowners were far more socially literate than he.

"It's 16:30," Enoch said. "Spit the rundown."

"Misty is out sick, but otherwise everything is running smoothly," the woman replied. "Currently eighty-seven patrons in the bar, nine staff, putting us twenty-four shy of capacity."

"It's a Thursday and it's early," Enoch said, leafing through papers. "Jus' make sure Biggs and Takeshi ain' pouring heavy and we'll turn a double profit."

"Also, I'm not sure whose fuck-up, but we got two cases of mezcal and none of tequila."

"*Hontō?*"

"Seriously."

"Eighty-six any tequila specials," Enoch said. "*Kihon* shit only."

The woman nodded, rising from the desk. She strode towards the door but stopped short.

"That's only half of business," she said. "But do you want me to tell you with him here?" She gestured to Chibi.

"Especially with him here," Enoch replied. "He's gon' be my new *hosa*."

"Has he earned his halo?"

"*Kuso*. Hell no," Enoch replied. "Barely a few feathers."

"Whatever," the woman said, shaking her head, "not my problem if he spills his guts."

Chibi was more confused than before. "Earning a halo" — what did that even mean? And what other business would there be to discuss? His heart sank, yet again wondering what the hell he had gotten into. He understood that this was his life now, and he was kind of stuck, but he still longed for a time he wouldn't feel so nervous about everything.

"Key is headed to a meeting with the Wires," the woman continued.

Wires? Chibi thought. *Why is that familiar?*

"Wires?" Enoch asked. "Tha's not a call I made."

"No," the woman agreed. "You didn't but we needed to meet with them."

"This just a face-to-face or is something shit brewin'?"

Chibi tried to follow the conversation, but he'd have to confess he was lost. He *knew* he knew "the Wires", but he couldn't place it. It's not like he spent a lot of time in the Cauldron before the last couple of days, so whatever business was being done, it was something he probably shouldn't have known about. Still, he couldn't shake the familiarity.

"You know as well as I do that the chrome-domes don't make trouble, but —"

"But they sure as hell get the pot stirrin'," Enoch interjected. "I don' want my main man walkin' into some shit because you moved without my green."

"It'll be fine."

Enoch got to his feet, a glimmer of rage in his eyes.

"Nat," he said. "I am the rules. I am *oyabun*. *I* run the Black Angels."

Black Angels.

Those words sent a chill down Chibi's spine. He was able to place where he remembered the Wires now.

Notorious Web Gang "the Wires" Hack Nu U Systems, Who Will Be Their Next Target?

"You guys are gangsters?" Chibi asked, not entirely conscious of having said the words out loud.

Enoch cracked a smile, though the flame didn't die in his eyes.

"Heard of us, *inu?*" he asked rhetorically. "*Hai*. Tha's us."

"You now, too," Nat added.

"Nah," Enoch said, cutting in again. "I just said he ain' got his halo."

"But you said —"

"Nat," Enoch spat, cutting her off, "go run my fucking bar."

Nat was clearly shocked, a bit upset, but she nodded, dropping her gaze, and strode wordlessly to the door. She'd barely closed it before Chibi spat out another question without thinking.

"Is this why Med-Sec is after Key?" he asked. "Is it because he's a gangster?"

"What do you think, *inu?*"

Chibi hadn't.

"Why you think we have the wall?" Enoch asked.

The question seemed to come out of nowhere. It took Chibi a second to change mental tracks.

"There are sidewalks through it, trains pop over it, but the wall's still there," Enoch said, guiding Chibi to the answer he was looking for. "So why's it there if it's not doing a thing?"

Chibi thought back to a few days ago on the train, staring at the wall. He thought about the dread he had felt about being on the wrong side.

"It's imaginary," Chibi answered.

"*Hai,*" Enoch affirmed. "*Masani.*"

Chibi looked into Enoch's glowing eyes — black sclera and orange iris giving an inhuman feeling to them. He looked at Enoch's arms, robotic from the elbow down on the left and shoulder on the right; they were gold and gunmetal black — a fashionable model Chibi remembered Nu U rolling out a few years ago. He looked at Enoch's piercings and pink hair. Nothing about him was meant to "fit in" with others. For years, Chibi had only seen black-haired, brown-eyed people with flesh and bone.

There'd be the occasional blonde or brunette, rarely someone with dark skin, but it was like everyone had become a cardboard cutout of everyone else. The same three suits were worn by every person in the office, man or woman: gray, blue, and black. Ladies just swapped the pants for a pencil skirt.

It wasn't like that here.

"The wall is jus' a line they drew," Enoch said. "Doesn't change nothin', jus' tells people where they belong — who their people are."

Chibi knew that was true, but he'd never thought about it like that. The wall was an object of fear.

"Long answer to the short question," Enoch said. "No. *Yakusoku* Med-Sec don't care what happens this side of the wall. Not unless there's money in it."

CHAPTER 12
NOT DYING TONIGHT

Key stood outside the garage. Nat was right, the place was called Supe Ups. Key had never actually paid attention to the name, he just knew where it was. He'd come a few times for intel on investigations; the Wires were second to few when it came to getting information. That's what the place was: a massive computer lab. It hadn't been a garage for a while.

Nothing left but to do it, Key thought, crossing the street.

He knocked on the door. An eye-level panel slid open.

"Whozit?"

"Key."

"Whatzit?"

"Black Angels business."

"Da boss be divin', an I know nuttin' 'boutz it."

"Are you guys not expecting me?" Key asked, a bit annoyed already. "I thought I was here for a pick-up or something."

"Don' know nuttin 'boutz it."

"Can you get your boss?" Key asked. "Alpha, right?"

"Boss Alpha big sleepin' — deadz," the man on the other side answered. "Beta runninz 'til we pick da new Alpha."

"Then get Beta!" Key shouted. "Or just open the damn door

so I can come in."

"No can do," the man insisted. "Da boss be divin', an I know nuttin' 'boutz nuttin' to do wit' Black Angels."

Key was fed up. He reared back with his strong leg and kicked the door open. The guy behind was knocked backwards, scurrying away on hands and knees as Key strode inside. A few guys — barely lucid — stood up and took notice. They all had three or four data ports on their heads, each with a wire or two hooked in. One man was still in his chair, headset on and wires running into all five of his data ports.

"Get him out," Key commanded.

He spoke to no one in particular, and that yielded no particular result. He turned to one of the chrome-domes, a tall and lanky man with a greasy mop of hair hanging all about his head, the data ports protruding like some type of horn.

"You," Key said, pointing. "Get Beta out of whatever dive he's in."

"Boss don't like getting waked," the man said, fear and wariness coloring his voice.

"Youz bring mo' guyz?" the doorman asked.

Key turned to see what he was talking about, just in time to see the doorway and three meters of wall around it explode in a ball of fire. The force of the blast knocked Key and all the other guys back as the whole garage quickly went up in flames. The chrome-domes screamed and howled in pain. Despite his body being ablaze, Beta did not move or utter a word.

Shit.

That was the only thought Key could muster as he tried to get to his feet. He made it to his knees when he saw four jackboots enter the building. A triple-tap here and a four-shot there, all the Wires were put down. One of the jackboots darted over to Key, pointing a gun at his face. Unfortunately, the guy was smart enough to stay out of reach.

"Are you Heihachi Hanamura?" the man shouted over the roar of the inferno.

"Who the hell!?" Key replied, barely able to keep himself from coughing to death from the smoke.

The jackboot gestured and another came and jabbed Key in the neck. He tried to take a swipe, but the jackboot was quick. Through stinging eyes, Key saw the jackboot put a tiny vial of what he assumed was his blood into a data deck. The jackboot with the deck nodded, the one with the gun nodding back.

BANG!

The shot hit one of the plates in Key's head, ricocheting off to the side. Blood trickled down his face, but he was otherwise unharmed. Didn't stop the immediate headache, though.

BANG! BANG! BANG!

Key fell to the ground, pain blossoming in his head and chest.

Two to the heart, one to the brain . . . he thought. *Good form.*

The two bullets in his chest might be a problem, but he was sure the one to his head had failed again. He was sure.

Not dying tonight, he thought. *No way in hell.*

The world grew dim as the flames consumed the building completely. The roof started to cave in as Key slipped away.

CHIBI HAD some very large things to think about and had to process them very quickly. Over the span of twenty-four hours, he had lost his job, dog, and home, been shot, become embroiled in some sort of manhunt, and now he had been recruited into a gang almost without his even being aware of it. He lost track of time as the thoughts swirled in his head. He might have been sitting in that chair for over an hour by the time he fished himself out of the mental spiral. It was more than his brain could deal with. That's when the panic set in.

"I'm a gangster . . ." Chibi murmured.

"Not yet, *inu,*" Enoch said. "Though probably soon."

"When were you guys going to tell me?" Chibi asked, voice still weak and afraid.

"Don' know," Enoch admitted. "It's jus' life for us, so we don' even think about it. It's *shigoto*."

"But . . . you're gangsters," Chibi repeated. "Criminals."

"What laws you see me break?"

"You guys stole two crates from Tango-Tec, right?"

A look of confusion briefly graced Enoch's face before he shook it off.

"No," Enoch said. "At least not really."

This did little to put Chibi at ease.

"They say we steal, but all we take is *gomi* — we're jus' takin' trash they already gone and got rid of. My *kazo* robbed a Tango-Tec dump for two crates of surplus. Problem is the *kaiju*-corp don't like other people havin' their shit even if they ain' usin' it."

"But you guys kill people, right?"

"Sometimes," Enoch confessed. "Shit gets all kinds of hairy — straight and curly — and you gotta make sure you walk away from it."

"And you're . . . okay with that?"

Enoch cocked an eyebrow. Chibi's heart plummeted to his feet and the color drained from his face. He looked at his hands. He had felt the weight of what he did to some extent, but the reality of his actions was only just hitting him.

"I killed a man . . ."

"Lot easier in the heat of the moment, *ne, inu?*" Enoch asked, sitting back in his chair. "Bit tougher when you gotta look at'cha self later."

Chibi nodded solemnly.

"I'd say you'll get used to it, but I doubt you're ever gonna," Enoch said. "Try your best to stay like that. Keep ya'self *muku*."

KNOCK KNOCK

An urgent pounding at the door put a stop to their chat. Moments later, a very androgynous individual in a plunging button-up and jacket burst in.

"Enoch, baby!" they shouted, "There's somethin' wrong: Key is flatlining!"

CHAPTER 13
IMPOSSIBLE NOTHING

Key came to surrounded by the rubble of Supe Ups. He had a splitting headache, and his face and clothes were caked in blood and burned to shit, but he was otherwise unharmed. He looked at the wounds in his chest and the burns on his body. It wasn't immediately clear how he was awake at all.

The hell . . .?

He rose from the ashen, burned husk of a garage, the scent of a charred building mixing with fried circuit boards and flesh. He clumsily hobbled through the wreckage, looking for something — anything to make his trip out here worthwhile. Everything was swallowed by the fire. A creeping suspicion began to crawl up his spine. The Wires claimed to know nothing about this meet up, and then Med-Sec showed up? And who the hell was Heihachi Hanamura? Key flicked on his uplink, hoping to find some answers in the web.

"Query: Heihachi Hanamura."

For the first time in the three years Key had been a Detective, the feed was blank.

"Query: Hanamura Heihachi."

Blank.

"Med-Sec Heihachi"

Blank.

Key tried a half dozen searches, but they all came back with zero results. There was no way in hell it was possible, but there he stood with that impossible nothing.

What is happening?

He sat down on the sidewalk, the rain pelting his burned, half-naked body a cold comfort. He decided to once again put his Detective brain to work.

"Heihachi. Med-Sec. Jackboots. Manhunt. DNA. Me."

Whoever Heihachi was, he was clearly important. Key couldn't be entirely certain, but it seemed probable that Med-Sec thought it was him. That would explain the alarm bells when he went to have his DNA checked against their databases, and why they took his blood in the garage. Heihachi must have been a really big deal, because Chibi got blacklisted just for associating with Key. On top of that, they must have wanted him to stay secret, otherwise they wouldn't have shot up the Wires and burned Supe Ups. That's *way* too much flash if all they wanted was to kill him. They were obviously trying to cover it up.

I need a nap.

He reached up to his temple, the display for his phone appearing in his eye. He was sure Enoch had gotten an update on his vital signs when everything went down, but a call sure wouldn't hurt.

Hope he'll give me a ride.

Bing ba-da-bing. Bing ba-da-bing.

Enoch tapped his temple as he scrambled to get some gear together. He froze completely when he saw the name on the call.

"Key!?" he shouted, "*Bakane* . . . what the hell happened!?"

"Not completely sure," Key confessed. "The Wires had no idea I was coming."

"The Wires got you flatlining?"

"Fuck no," Key spat. "Some Med-Sec jackboots rocked up and torched the place. Shot us all up."

"Think it was payback for their hack on Nu U?"

"Maybe," Key answered. "What did you mean 'flatlined'?"

"One of the *otonan* told me you were flat," Enoch said. "Guess it was a mistake."

"Must be," Key said, a hint of doubt in his voice.

The two men were quiet, Key thinking and Enoch simply relieved to have been wrong about his death. Chibi, meanwhile, stood in stunned and complete silence through the entirety of the call. From the moment he heard Key's name, he froze.

"I'll get a car runnin' your way," Enoch said. "They'll take you home."

RATHER THAN GO HOME, Key had the driver take him to Six's clinic. Though he lived, he certainly wasn't loving the full-body burns and bullet wounds.

"What the hell happened!?" Six shrieked, all but dragging her husband to a bed.

She laid him down, darting around the room to assemble a treatment tray.

"I'm not entirely sure," Key admitted. "I was going to see the Wires — Nat said it was a routine meet-up — and then we were getting gunned down and set on fire."

"Nat sent you on the job?" Six asked skeptically.

"She told me about it. Obviously, I assumed she got the go-ahead from Enoch."

"Fucking idiot bitch," Six grumbled.

She cut off Key's clothes, applying white, gridded sheets to his burned skin.

"What're you thinking, Six?" Key asked, trying to distract himself from the pain.

"Sounds to me like she set you up," Six said, pulling the bullets from Key's chest. "You and I both know Med-Sec doesn't come over here without an invitation."

"Enoch thinks it might have been retaliatory," Key explained. "The price to be paid for that hack they pulled on Nu U."

"Is that what you think?" Six asked.

"No," Key confessed. "They were after something. Hunting someone named Heihachi Hanamura — and they seemed to think it was me."

Six slowed. Her movements became more deliberate as she grabbed the vita-light and hovered over the burns. Key could see her gaze grow distant as she mulled something over.

"Do you think they're right?" she asked.

"Hell if I know," Key replied. "But they seemed pretty convinced. Took a blood sample and everything."

"I assume you already checked the web," Six said, still a bit out of it. "Find anything?"

"Nothing. Like actual nothing."

"That's impossible." Six brushed the statement off. "Even if it's not what you wanted, there's no way there was literally nothing about someone named Heihachi Hanamura."

"I'm telling you, Six, there was nothing. Whoever it is, me or not, it's a black hole of information."

"Still don't buy it. Someone is messing with you or something."

"Seems suspect, that's for sure," Key said. "I guess I'll find someone to dig through the deep web and see if they can turn anything up."

"You mean Gode. You're going to talk to Gode."

"Yeah. I know you hate him, but he's the best source of info in the Cauldron."

"Because he's a traitorous snake that has no allegiances."

"You're not wrong . . ." Key admitted. "But this is the second time in only a few days someone has tried to kill me. I can't afford to drag my feet."

CHAPTER 14
FISH CAN TURN INTO DRAGONS

A couple of days went by as Chibi continued his "job" as Enoch's assistant. He hadn't gone back to his apartment — not much point — and he doubted anyone was missing him. He hadn't talked to his parents in months, and he was just a lurking ghost everywhere else.

It seemed he was going to be spending a while living with Six and Key, bumming it on their couch and working for Enoch. It wasn't a bad gig; it mostly constituted following Enoch around while he talked to people, which was easy if a bit boring. Honestly, Chibi was glad to have a job that didn't keep him sitting behind a desk.

"You wanna get your halo?" Enoch asked.

The question came as a surprise. It wasn't like they had been talking about the Black Angels or anything, so Chibi certainly wasn't prepared with an answer. Did he?

"Um . . ." he paused.

"I know you been a *shironai* all your life, but I think you've got the right shape to fit this puzzle."

"I want to belong."

The words spilled out of his mouth before he processed them, but they weren't wrong. He'd been cast out of his old life and alienated in his new one. If becoming a Black Angel meant he got to be a part of something bigger — a community — something he'd missed for long enough he lost count of the years, he was at least open to it.

"I'm not sure about being a Black Angel or whatever, but I want to do more than follow you around."

"Gotta keep the *shironai* as *shiro* as possible, *ne?*"

"Something like that."

"Seems to me like you ain' ready to commit," Enoch said. "You tied a knot and you ain' ready to unravel it."

"Maybe not," Chibi admitted, "but I don't want to be sidelined, either."

Enoch stood from his desk, gesturing for Chibi to follow.

BLOCK AFTER BLOCK, the two men walked for a while, Enoch not saying a word. Chibi was confused, but he also had no idea what to say. The conversation had ended pretty abruptly, but he doubted Enoch was leading him nowhere. He elected to trust the walk. Enoch's somber silence did concern him, though.

Where are we going?

The two came to the Rokutsu River, snaking its way through the city. Aside from Nanashishi Park in the heart of Hajishin, the river was the only organic thing left. Sure, there were trees planted in parks and some buildings had atriums or greenhouses, but it was all manufactured to give the *idea* of nature; it wasn't the real thing. The Rokutsu, though, was the real thing. You could fish in the water or go swimming outside the city. Chibi had always seen it through more cynical eyes. He felt like the city choked the life out of the planet. For some reason, on this random afternoon, it hit him differently. Chibi sat on the wall — there was no riverbank in the city — and gazed into the dark water and saw the lights of the city dance. He was mesmerized by the shimmer and shadows of fish moving through the water.

"You know, *inu*, there's a story about this city."

Chibi didn't respond, simply staring into the water. Enoch took a long draw off his cigarette, blowing the wispy smoke into the air.

"Story goes, when the Singularity starting popping in the cosmos, the fish of Rokutsu-*sama* changed." Enoch continued. "They got claws and fangs — started growin' legs."

Enoch took a seat next to Chibi.

"They got *kyodi* — massive — and real long," Enoch said, his voice soft. "After a while, they got smart, too, and they crawled out of the river."

Chibi imagined the sight. Fish transforming and taking to land. It had been a while since he'd daydreamed like this. He had kind of missed it.

"They called themselves *Ryū*, and they built an empire."

Enoch lifted his gaze to the sky.

"When the first Empyreans arrived on Galivaria, ready to subjugate the world, the *Ryū* were gone. Some say the *henka* never stopped — they kept growing and changing and flew into space to live among the stars. Other people say they fled back to Rokutsu-*sama*."

"You're saying there's dragons in the river?" Chibi asked.

"Maybe," Enoch replied. "Tha's not my point, though."

"What are you trying to say?"

"I'm sayin' that if fish can turn into dragons, you can grow into something more than a pencil-pushing *shironai, ne?*"

The idea hit Chibi hard. Sure, he'd considered being more than a salary worker for some tech giant. He had wanted to accomplish something big and special, but he fell short of it. Then, he kept settling. He'd never actually had someone encourage him to be more than he was.

"What should I become, then?"

"Tha's up to you, *kazo*."

CHAPTER 15
DON'T DO ANYTHING STUPID

A week passed, much to Key's chagrin, but Six insisted. All told, a week to heal from being shot four times and trapped in a fire was nothing to sneeze at.

The wonders of medical technology, he thought.

Still, he wanted nothing more than to go out and keep chasing the leads he had. Every turn brought more questions, but he couldn't help the chase. Though with how tired his burn treatments made him, he was also glad for the rest. After a week, he could still nap on command.

Chibi walked in the door, spotting Six on the couch.

"Heard Key was about done with treatment," he said, a somewhat encouraging note to his voice.

"Yeah," Six replied solemnly.

"What's up?" Chibi asked. "You sound almost disappointed."

"I am."

The reply shocked Chibi. He came around to sit on the coffee table, their positions reversed from the night they met.

"Key is alive," Chibi said. "He's safe."

"But for how long?" Six asked. "You don't understand, I've

been dealing with this for three years, Chibi. Three years I've watched him do this."

"He's been okay so far."

"Bullshit," Six spat. "I've put him and the other Angels back together a dozen times each."

"Why don't you ask him to stop?"

"I always thought he'd hit a wall eventually," she confessed. "I definitely thought this tangle with Med-Sec would make him back off."

"Key doesn't strike me as a guy who slows down easy," Chibi said. "Nor is he a guy that's super open about what he thinks."

Six sighed, rising from the couch. "Go to sleep, Chibi. I'll try to get you a futon this week."

She strode to her room without another word, leaving him alone. He moved to the couch, laying his head on his folded arm. It was strange, he'd spent so long terrified of becoming a Sundowner, but now that he was one, it was the Sundowners who seemed to reject him.

Earn your place, he thought. *Just like anything else.*

Gurgle.

Chibi's stomach growled. He realized he hadn't eaten since breakfast. Things had gotten so crazy, he'd only just noticed how long it had been since he ate. Famished, he got up from the couch and walked into the kitchen. He was pretty sure he remembered where everything was, but figured Jeeves would help if needed.

"Katsu."

That was what he had his mind set on. He wanted a delicious, succulent, breaded pork steak. He honestly couldn't help but salivate at the thought. Alas, upon opening the refrigerator, he was greeted with no pork. There were eggs, sure. There was plenty of milk — an ungodly amount of milk — and two bottles of chocolate syrup, a tub of tuna salad, and a massive bowl of leftover rice, but no pork steaks. He opened the freezer to find the same lack of pork. He wasn't sure if the apartment even had an Insta-thaw, but he figured it was worth looking, anyway.

Damn.

Hopes dashed, he decided to search the pantry for something else. Touching the panel on the wall, the pantry door slid open, revealing copious cereals and canned coffee, but nothing to satisfy his umami craving. There *were* some shrimp chips. He decided to settle.

Plopping back on the couch, shrimp chips in hand, he dug in. In truth, he was hungry enough that it didn't much matter what he ate, it was going to be delicious regardless. He hadn't looked at a clock all day, and he spent a good chunk of it passed out, but Chibi *felt* like it was far too early to go to bed. Not that it had stopped the happy couple.

"Jeeves?" he called. "What time is it?"

"The time is 22:37, sir," the AI replied. "One hour and twenty-three minutes to midnight."

Bit later than I thought.

Still, sleep wasn't about to take him. He propped his feet up on the coffee table, still munching on the shrimp chips.

"Turn on the TV, Jeeves," he said.

The glossy black void clicked to life. His TV at home hadn't worked for months. Granted, he also hadn't been awake past 20:00 in over a year. Work, drink, sleep. Work, drink, sleep. That had been his routine ever since he got the job at Kigen. He used to think it was great to live such a simple life, but it drained him quickly. After that, he'd just settled into his rhythm. It wasn't like he hadn't tried to change it up. He went on a date or two and used his apartment's Smart Gym 360 for a sporadic few months, but a well-travelled path has deep grooves; his changes never lasted long. He reached out for his beloved shiba to hop up next to him.

Oh . . .

How quickly he'd forgotten. There'd been so much else going on, he had yet to notice the glaring absence. His arm dropped to the couch, lifeless. Any comfort he'd found in the chips and the glow of the TV faded, replaced by hollow longing. He dropped the bag, likely spilling chips all over the floor, but he didn't notice. He slowly lay on his side, drawing his feet up as he curled into a ball.

Chibi . . .

He cried himself to sleep.

COME MORNING, Chibi awoke to the smell of bacon. He sat up to see Key standing in the kitchen, shirtless, back to him as he cooked up breakfast. His derm patches were gone and his skin looked good as new. It was the first time Chibi had been able to properly see Key's piecemealed body. A dull, gray discoloration under the skin of his back must be his spine. Pale scar tissue covered the center of his back, from base to hairline. Around the center of his lumbar, thoracic, and cervical spine, small studs protruded from the skin. They may have been ports, but Chibi didn't know enough about prosthetics to say for sure. Extending almost all the way to the center, certainly past his shoulder blades, were his prosthetic arms.

Chibi watched, somewhat mesmerized, as the artificial muscles extended and contracted. As far as overall shape, the arms were nothing extraordinary. They were crafted to resemble those of a well-toned athlete. On a normal person, they might have looked out of place, but Key's flesh was as fit as his machines. Were it not for the fact they were gunmetal black — and the copious scars surrounding them — Chibi wouldn't have been surprised at all to learn that they weren't prosthetic at all. The same could be said of his leg. Despite only one being prosthetic, both legs looked identical, well-formed and strong.

Bang bang bang.

Someone was at the door. The knocking wasn't overly loud, but a metal door would never be particularly quiet, either.

"Get the door, Jeeves," Key called without turning from the stove.

The door slid open and in walked a two-and-a-half-meter-tall robot. Chibi was given pause, looking the robot over. It was tall, sure, ducking to clear the doorway, but it wasn't what he would consider "large." Rather, the robot was quite lanky, it's legs and arms more function than form. Its head was more or less the shape of a bucket with a single rectangular eye in the center. At least Chibi thought it was an eye.

"Were you followed?" Key asked.

"You really think someone followed me?" the robot asked. "Everyone assumes I'm a service-bot or something."

Chibi stared. The robot turned to look at him.

"Who's the squib?"

Key chuckled, still not turning.

"Ajax, this is Chibi," he said. "Chibi, Ajax."

"Sup." Ajax folded his arms.

"You're awfully articulate for a robot," Chibi said curiously.

"That's cause I'm not," Ajax corrected. "Way to profile machine lifeforms."

"Then you're —"

"An Oran," Ajax interjected. "Yeah."

Chibi had never met an Oran before, though he'd certainly heard about them. They were all over the news for their protests across the Empyrean Union to get the same rights as flesh-and-blood mortals. There were plenty on Mars, Empyrea Prime, and the mining colonies on the fringe of the Near Reach, but they were a rarity on Galivaria. Chibi had never really considered it, but it was strange that the leading world for biotech development had such issues with the Orans. It probably had something to do with their origins being so clouded in mystery. Were they robots given sentience by the Singularity? Were they souls, born of the Akashic, inhabiting the physical forms of machines? No one knew. And people don't much care for the unknown.

"So . . ." Chibi said awkwardly. "What brings you?"

"He's going to help me investigate this Heihachi Hanamura guy," Key answered, finally sitting down with his meal. "Whoever he is, any info about him has been scrubbed — or at least made secret — so my searches using my uplink aren't turning over any stones. He's basically been erased from the public record. I've been down too long, so you, me, and Six are gonna go talk to a guy I know in the Underground while Ajax does some snooping of his own."

Chibi got up from the couch, accidently crushing spilled shrimp chips as he walked to the table. Key stared at the bag of chips on the floor then looked, irritated, at Chibi.

"Six is *not* cleaning that up."

As if conjured by her name, Six emerged from the bedroom. She looked surprised by the Oran, but not put off by him.

"I didn't realize Key had asked you over," she said, patting Ajax on the arm. "It's good to see you."

"Good to see you, too," Ajax answered. "It's been a while."

"Eight months," Key said. "Since she said I wasn't supposed to reach out to you anymore and stuff."

"He got you stabbed," Six said, accusingly glancing at Ajax, then Key.

"Only through the arm," Key argued. "And you fixed it!"

"I attached a new arm," Six corrected. "You took our debt to Doc from 200,000 to 340,000 jul!"

Chibi's eyes widened. He knew prosthetics were expensive — he'd spent years doing price calculations for them — but he'd never really had those numbers put in context before. He had only made 220,000 last *year*. Paying off prosthetics was insane.

"He's gouging us and you know it," Key spat. "A hundred and forty thousand for this arm was robbery." He held up his right arm. "If two arms, a leg, and my eyes cost two hundred, how the hell does one arm cost one-forty?"

"Didn't realize I was opening a wound . . ." Ajax said, slowly backing away.

"Don't you go anywhere," Six said, pointing at Ajax. "Just . . . don't do anything stupid."

Her eyes filled with tears. She tried to quickly wipe them away but couldn't stop them coming. Holding back sobs, she went to the bathroom, closing the door behind her. A heavy and awkward silence fell over the room. With a cough and a final bite of food, Key got up from the table.

"I'll just go . . . handle that," he said, walking towards the bathroom door.

Ajax nodded his bucket head and motioned for Chibi to follow. At least, Chibi was pretty sure. With no facial expressions and only four fingers per hand, it was hard to make out Ajax's intentions. Either way, Chibi rose from the table, following Ajax out front.

KEY KNOCKED on the bathroom door. He could hear the shower running and Six crying, but the door wouldn't open. He got no reply.

"Open the door, Jeeves."

"I'm sorry, sir, but the madame has locked it."

"I know that," Key answered, frustrated. "I want you to unlock it."

"I'm sorry, sir, but I don't have privileges to override an administrator's lock."

"I'm an administrator!" Key yelled. "Open the damn door, you half-assed butler!"

The door opened, Six standing in front of it. She was half-clothed, and her eyes were wet and red. Key stepped into the bathroom, closing the door behind him. Six didn't speak, finishing her undressing and climbing into the shower, pulling the curtain closed.

"I'm sorry, Six," Key said, voice heavy.

So many emotions swirled in his head, he wasn't even sure what he felt. Definitely regret. He regretted all the reckless shit he'd done over the last three years, both in pursuit of his past and just in general. He regretted how little he considered the impact that losing him might have on her. He felt lost. He had caught a trail — tasted his past, and the flavor was bitter — yet he couldn't stop himself from pursuing it further. He didn't know why. He didn't know what drove him, but he simply couldn't leave the past alone. He refused. He had to know.

"Talk to me," he pleaded.

She said nothing. Key walked over to the tub, stopping shy of grabbing the curtain. His hand hovered a breath away as he hesitated. Was he wrong to chase his past? Would he even know the man he found? Would he want to? Feeling regretful and directionless were nothing if he didn't do something with them. He had to actually consider the impact; he had to think bigger.

"Can I come in?"

Six said nothing, but the curtain opening a little gave him his answer. Not even bothering to take off the shorts he'd slept in, Key climbed into the shower. Six stood, finally breaking into full sobs as the water cascaded over her head. Key couldn't tell the tears from the water, but it didn't matter much. He took a half step forward, wrapping Six in his arms. She clutched her hands to her chest, crying against Key's.

"Why am I not enough?" she wept. "Why can't I be enough?"

It was like an arrow through Key's chest.

"I . . ."

He had no explanation he felt would satisfy her. Plagued by sleepless nights, driven to the edge of sanity by dreams, it all made sense to him, but he couldn't guarantee it would to anyone else.

"I fell in love with the brash, fearless man you are *now,*" she cried. "Why do you want to be anything more than that?"

Key's heart pounded in his chest. He looked deep within himself and knew he had to tell her about the nightmares — fragments of the past that left him drained and more exhausted than when he went to bed. After three years of this, he owed her that much.

"I get these little splinters . . ." Key murmured, "pieces of memory that get stuck in my head. I sleep all the time, but my dreams . . . they suck the life out of me." He looked to Six, swallowing the lump in his throat. "I have to find the past — put it to rest — so that *I* can finally rest."

"I always knew you'd be your own downfall," Six said, the sobs fading, "but I never considered what that meant."

Key felt a wave of guilt wash over him. She fell in love with him for his fearlessness — his willingness to stare danger in face — but that was the very thing that nearly got him killed. What was to keep his next brush with death from being his last?

"I'm sorry," Key said.

It was small in the face of all he had to atone for, but it was all he had.

"I watched you die three times on my operating table," Six said. "I won't do it again."

She wrapped her arms around him, her body radiating warmth and comfort.

She's wrong, he thought. *She is enough.*

"I have no intention of dying again," he said. "But I can't just leave this alone anymore, either. If I don't put the old me in the ground, it'll kill me first."

"I know," Six said. "You chased it too long, and now the past is reaching back."

It was true. If he'd stopped a month ago, he could have lived in peace. Sure, there were the dreams, fragments of memories, and the past may have *eventually* caught up with him, but there was no guarantee of that. Now . . . now he'd opened Pandora's

Box. He uncovered something — or something uncovered him — and people were hunting him. There's no way Med-Sec was operating on their own; they were always serving someone else's ends; meaning he had much bigger enemies who were yet to reveal themselves.

"I promise," Key said, voice shaking, "I'm not going to die."

"You can't promise that," Six said, releasing him from her embrace, "but I'm holding you to it anyway."

The couple sat down in the shower, leaning back in the tub as the water fell down on them. Key kissed Six's head, closing his eyes. He couldn't be sure what was to come, who he'd face, and what awaited on the other side, but he had that moment. Free from fear and regret, he had that blissful moment of peace.

OUT FRONT, the rain was just a slight misting. It was the lightest precipitation they'd had in weeks. Chibi rarely took notice of the weather since he spent ninety-eight percent of his time indoors, but he'd been paying more attention the last couple days. He wasn't sure why he suddenly cared about the rain, but then a lot of things had changed.

"What's your story?" Ajax asked. "You're dressed like Enoch, and that plate on your head is hardly 'socially acceptable', but you're certainly not a Sundowner."

"I am, I guess," Chibi said quietly. "But I haven't been for long."

"What happened?" Ajax asked.

"I stepped out of place." He looked up to the gray sky. "I was on the train, coming home from work, when I saw two guys arguing." He shoved his hands in his pockets, breathing deeply and sighing. "One guy shot at the other and they took off. I chased them."

"Why?"

"Dunno," Chibi answered absently, "I guess I was bored. I

didn't have anything pressing to go home to — no one counting on me — so I decided to follow them."

"Mistake," Ajax said.

"I know. But I did it anyway."

It was true he was bored; his life was hollow. Still, chasing after an armed man and a fugitive wasn't something your everyday salaryman did. He was just so desperate to break out of the rut he was in. Daydreams could only keep him satiated for so long.

"Turned out the guy with the gun had friends," Chibi continued, "and his friends blew up the train."

"Damn."

"I survived the crash, but the guys in black were none too happy about that, so they plugged me in the head," Chibi said, placing a finger-gun to his temple.

"That how you got the plate?"

"Nah," Chibi said. "But the plate *is* what saved my life. That and Key dragging me back here."

"Key was the guy getting chased."

Chibi nodded.

"He carried me back here and Six fixed me up."

"That sounds like them," Ajax said. "Seems like Key is always running. Doesn't matter if he's running towards something or away from it, he can't sit still."

"I've noticed."

"He's a great guy, don't get me wrong, he's just . . . restless."

"Is Six always cleaning up his mess?" Chibi asked.

"More or less." Ajax shrugged. "It's their dynamic."

Chibi held out his hand, cupping the rain drops that dripped from the awning. The rain was cold, but he didn't mind.

"As long as I've known them, that's just how it is," Ajax said. "He's the brash, emotional one, and she's the calm thinker. They balance each other; it works."

"I can't be too disparaging," Chibi confessed, "I owe them

both my life." He took the rain in his hand and splashed it on his face. "What's your story?"

"Not much," Ajax replied. "Pretty standard among my kind."

"What's that? I confess you're the first Oran I've met."

"I woke up in a scrap heap," Ajax answered. "Both my legs were gone, but I had my arms. Took some time, but I figured out how to move my body."

Ajax held up his hands, looking them over, front and back.

"I crawled around, legless, for a while before some people found me," he said, lowering his arms. "They were . . . not great people."

Chibi turned to look at Ajax. Even without a face, Chibi could tell he was sad.

"They gave me legs on the condition that I'd be a Battle Bot," Ajax continued. "I did that for a while, but they never really treated me like a person — I was an object for their entertainment."

Chibi reached out and touched Ajax's arm.

"I refused to fight, so they took my arms and legs," Ajax said, voice betraying what his face could not. "They threatened to fry my chip if I didn't fight anymore."

"Your chip?"

Ajax nodded. "Despite the fact that we are *way* more complicated than robots, the Oran is still tied to the motherboard. That's what allows us to change out our parts." His countenance fell, shoulders slumping and head hanging. "It's also what makes us mortal."

"Oh . . ." Chibi murmured. "So, they were going to kill you."

Ajax nodded again. "So . . . I fought," he admitted. "To save my life."

"That's nothing to be ashamed of."

"You're right," Ajax said. "And I never fought another Oran."

"How'd you get out of that?" Chibi asked. "*Are* you out of that?"

"Yeah," Ajax said, voice brightening. "The Black Angels had

a bit of a tiff with the guys that had me, so I ended up getting free from them."

Black Angels . . . Chibi thought. *Always heard they were menaces to society, but . . . seems not.*

"I'm not one of them," Ajax said, "but they're definitely my friends."

"You and Key are like kindred spirits, huh?"

Ajax chuckled. "I guess so, yeah. We both woke up in a scrap heap, torn limb from limb with no memory of life before that moment."

"Do you like being an Oran?" Chibi asked.

"I didn't have much of a choice," Ajax responded. "But I'll say this: it's hard."

"How so?"

"To never sleep . . . to have no feeling or taste . . . it's lonely. It's . . . isolating."

"Is there anything you could do?" Chibi asked, "I thought you guys could like upgrade and stuff."

"We can," Ajax confessed, "but doing it's expensive. People don't just throw away a full android body like yesterday's soup."

Chibi clenched a fist, holding it up to eye level. "I want to help you," he said.

"What?"

"I want to help you get a new body."

"Why?" Ajax asked, touched but confused. "You just met me."

"Because," Chibi said, "I can't do much to help Key with his issues. I'd probably just get in the way. But I used to work for Kigen. I know all kinds of stuff about how to get your get your hands on . . . hands."

Both laughed at the joke. It was weak, but it broke the tension. Ajax held out for a handshake.

"You've got a deal."

AFTER LEAVING Ajax at the apartment, Key and Six led Chibi down a flight of stairs and into the Underground. Chibi had long heard stories of what people did in the — effectively ancient — subway tunnels. No one had used the tunnels for trains in over a hundred and fifty years, making them perfect hives for scum and villainy. Those were the stories Chibi heard. His classmates in school told tales about wide-eyed nocturnals prowling about, high on myriad substances that made them little more than animals, and cannibal gangs that ate those who dared trespass in their territory. It sent a shiver down Chibi's spine even then, though he was sure the fear was pointless.

The Underground was dark — unsurprising given that the city had cut the electricity long ago — but Chibi heard voices coming from further down the tunnel. The main problem with the subway tunnels was the flooding, turning the tracks into subterranean canals. Chibi saw light dancing on the surface of the water.

"Come on," Key said, dragging a raft from the platform to the water.

Curious, Chibi got in, Key paddling the three of them past what Chibi realized to be a post-abandonment wall built by whoever now occupied the station. After rowing thirty meters or so, they were able to see the source of light and voices: a metaverse den. Bars of blacklights illuminated the walls — as much as blacklights can — causing the weathered, white-and-blue tiles to glow vibrantly. Seven massive black boxes pulsed with rainbow light, cables running to the seven chairs placed between them. More accurately, they ran to the headsets of the people in the chairs. Two were empty, their intended occupants sitting at a table on the far side of the room, talking. They must have heard the soft splash of the paddle, for they fell silent and turned to the newcomers.

"Who dares approach my domain?" one of them asked, rising from the table.

"Come on, Nekros," Key complained, "let us pass."

Chibi could tell by the guy's bone structure he'd been attractive once. But alas, since he rarely went aboveground and clearly subsisted on nutria bars and an IV, his face and body looked gaunt from malnutrition.

"You speak my name without announcing yourself!?" Nekros shrieked.

"Nekros, honey," Six said. "It's Six and Key."

"Then who is this foul third?" Nekros demanded. "Some demon bent on destroying all that lies beyond?"

"This is Chibi," Six explained. "He's a friend of ours."

Nekros puzzled over this, his skeletal face struggling to form an expression.

"Very well," he said. "Speak the words of passage and you shall be free."

Key sighed. "Ababheki. Ere di ohia. Makabati menesada. Ovo te amedera, taime ere opus."

Nekros smiled and nodded. "You may pass."

"Thank you, Nekros, Lord of the Avernus Passage," Six said. "May all who pass bless you."

Nekros bowed and returned to the table as Key resumed rowing. After they were far enough away, Chibi decided to ask a few questions.

"Who was that?"

"Nekros," Key answered, laughing to himself. "He's a harmless enough guy. He was a financier once, but the death of his parents shook him really bad. After that, he got *way* too deep into the metaverse — just trying to escape, I think — and lost his job, house, everything."

"So that's why he lives in the Underground?"

"Kind of," Six said. "He's just retreated so far into his fantasy that he'd rather pretend to be an arbiter of the magical canal than face the real world."

Chibi thought about that. He thought about how easily he could have ended up the same way. He had already started, hiding from his numbing misery by isolating himself from the world. At least Nekros had friends around him.

"I see no harm in indulging him," Key said. "Even if it's mildly inconvenient."

CHAPTER 16
THAT BLISSFUL MOMENT

After rowing past more stations, some large and sprawling — turned to generator-lit communities for those who couldn't afford the apartments above — and some little more than a wider section of tunnel someone had elected to tile, the raft came to a gate blocking the way.

"Shit," Key muttered.

"What?" Chibi asked.

"Gimme the gun," Six said, holding her hand out to Key.

He drew his pistol, passing it back to her as he braced for conflict. It was dark, but his eyes had no trouble with that.

"Open the gate!" he yelled into the black.

All at once, a dozen lights flicked on, their beams shining at the raft. The sudden change blinded Key, his eyes flooded with pure white. They whirred, dilating and fine-tuning but unable to adjust to the harsh lighting.

"No can do, Angel," a mystery voice said from the shadows. "You're not supposed to be alive anymore. Seems the job got botched. We aim to fix that."

"The tunnels are neutral, you fucks," Key growled. "Now open the gate so that we can keep going."

He pulled off his blue-gray hooded jacket, an angel with no

head but many eyes on the back — a symbol of his role and allegiance. Dread set in. He looked back at his companions, barely able to make out the stoic determination on Six's face and the abject horror on Chibi's. Chibi opened his mouth, but Key shook his head.

"Do you guys really want to start this?" he asked wearily.

"Start and finish," the voice said.

"Knowing full well that I'm a Detective, and who I work for?"

"Med-Sec put a price on your head," the voice answered. "We're going to cash in."

Key was taken aback a moment.

Price on my head?

He didn't have time to think that over yet.

"How good is your night-sight?" Key asked.

"What?"

"You heard the damn question."

"I don't —"

The man never finished his sentence. Key jumped from the raft to the platform, landing a fist in the guy's face. Panic spread through the group as they tried to strike back, but they couldn't land their hits. Now out of the oppressive beams of the floodlights, returned to the dark, Key could see again, bobbing and weaving around the platform. A few of his opponents drew guns, firing at him, briefly illuminating the station. He spotted six or seven guys, all trying desperately to take him down. They failed. Bullets made contact, but none could penetrate; there were certainly perks to having a shit-ton of metal in your body. With naught but fists — albeit bionic ones — Key dispatched them, knocking over their floodlights in the process and bathing the entire tunnel in black. As the last fell, Key stood, bloody and a little worse for wear, standing over the battered corpses of his fellow combatants.

"Damn . . ." Chibi murmured.

Key flipped a switch, causing the gate to whir and grind as it descended into the water. He got back in the raft, taking up the paddle without remark. No one else said a word, the only sound the gentle lapping of the water against the boat.

AFTER ROWING for what must have been a few kilometers, the canal came to an end. Rather than a simple wall, however, it opened up into a massive lake. What was once the train depot, the nest from which all the steel behemoths emerged, scattering across the myriad lines of rail, had become flooded like all the rest. It wasn't as grand as something like Miyazaki Central — the golden, resplendent station where all the high-rails converged — but its size was undeniable. There were even remnants of the old system in the form of rusted husks of trains, filled halfway by the rain. Dimly lit by what must have been generators, it had a slightly eerie quality, as if the lake were haunted by the trains themselves. Yet for all the tingling on Chibi's skin, there was still a beauty to it. A cluster of three vents near the center of the domed ceiling allowed fresh air to flow into the room, unlike the stagnant, musty air of the other stations — save for a few. Moreover, it allowed the rain to flow in from outside, causing a cascading waterfall near the center of the lake. Mist shimmered in the low light and cast rainbows over the water.

"Chibi," Six said.

Chibi looked at her, realizing the raft had docked. Key was already up on the platform, as was Six, both waiting for him to exit. He stumbled a little as the raft shifted but made his way without falling into the murk below. He wouldn't have sworn to it, but he thought he saw a shark in the water.

Key took the lead, navigating through a series of hallways. The depot must have also served as a sort of central office for the Department of Rail and Road, given the size and number of rooms. At one point, they were surely offices, but now they were empty. Still, the bureaucratic soul of the place lived on. When they got to the end of the hall, they came to what must have been the department head's office. The door was much nicer, and the location allowed it to be significantly larger than the rest. From under the door came the glow of a lamp.

"Let me do the talking first," Key said.

Chibi nodded as he opened the door, the three of them filing in. Sitting on the opposite side of an ornate desk was a man with wrinkled, sickly green skin and slick, oily hair. His eyes were like goggles surgically implanted in his skull, and he had no nose to speak of. After a second or two, Key caught the man's smell, holding back a groan.

"Gode," he said.

"Key," the man replied, voice oddly high and raspy.

The two locked eyes for a moment, wordlessly sizing each other up.

"I asked for intel and you said you had it," Key said. "Spill."

Gode coughed — a heavy cough like that of a thirty-year smoker.

"I heardyou was tryna fig'r out who was sendin' jackboots after ya."

"Yes," Key said.

"I also heard you went to the fuggin' cops — the goddamned, mutha fuggin' *law* — foist," Gode muttered. "Enoch, too."

"They're good friends to have."

"I'm the info man!" Gode yelled, sending himself into a coughing fit. "You want the good shit, you best come to me foist, else you'll see how I hold onto my title through the thick and the skinny!"

"I'm here," Key said, waiting for Gode to stop coughing. "I

know that when I want the whispers and secrets, I need to come to you. You've got the hackers, the deep web connections, I get it." He took a deep breath, calming himself. "I got my topside knowledge; now I want the underground stuff. So, what do you have for me?"

Gode stared skeptically, scratching at his chin. "I been hearin' whispers 'bout *who* the jackboots 're goin' after," he said after a long minute.

Key said nothing, simply crossing his arms.

"Ya want the good deets, ya best pay," Gode snarled.

"I already know who they're after," Key replied. "Some guy named Heihachi Hanamura. The problem is the guy's been erased from the web completely." He braced his hands on the desk, assuming a more threatening stance. "Tell me something I don't know."

Gode sat back in his chair, seemingly unfazed by Key's posturing.

"Word travels fast in the Underground y'know," Gode said, applying his own brand of pressure. "Heard that not even an hour ago, ya put down a few o' the Fifth Sector boys."

"And what if I did?"

"It'd be a shame if Tengu learned that the Black Angels drew blood, wouldn't it?" Gode asked patronizingly. "I mean, you'se might be a pretty strong bunch, but there's only twelve a ya, and there's sixty-some o' them. Not to mention the price Med-Sec got on you."

"I'll worry about the consequences of my own actions," Key said. "You worry about making sure I didn't come all the way over here for nothing."

"I want my pay foist," Gode said. "Otherwise —"

He was interrupted by a blade at his throat. Key grabbed him by the collar, dragging him onto the desk as he placed the edge of his knife to Gode's disgusting skin.

"Are you threatening me?" Key growled. "Because I'll

remind you who has the legal protection for slitting your throat right now."

"Okay, okay!" Gode cried, all air of pretense evaporating.

Key released him, sliding the knife back into its place on the back of his belt. Gode adjusted himself, trying to regain his composure. Were it not for the fact that Gode already smelled like the underside of a dumpster, he'd have sworn the goblin-man pissed himself.

"Obviously, y'know they's afta Heihachi and what the fuggin' eva," Gode said. "But ya don' know *who* they's afta."

Key rolled his eyes, considering his knife again. "The hell do you mean?"

"I mean you's got da name, but you don' know who dat is."

"Obviously," Key retorted. "That's why I asked you. Are you honestly saying that the Underground has nothing on this?"

"I know your name."

Key's blood went cold. He tried to hide the combination of panic and elation that danced in his heart and head. He must have failed to conceal his thoughts, as Gode began to laugh uncontrollably, nearly sending himself into another coughing fit.

"I knew I could pique ya int'rest," he said. "Ya been chasin the past fa what . . . two yea's?"

Key stayed silent, not trusting himself to speak.

"Well, I been hearin' bout a guy wit a synth spine they's been tryna find," Gode continued, "Them's pretty rare, and hella fuckin' expensive, so there's only one guy *I* know 'round 'ere tha's got one."

Key felt Six touch his back. It was comforting, but he couldn't keep his voice from trembling.

"I know."

"I also been hearin' these same folks talkin' 'bout people disappearin' after they sta'ted havin' issues wit they bionics."

"What is my name?" Key asked, trying to get the conversation back on topic. "Am I Heihachi?"

"Don' ca'a 'bout the folks losin' they limbs, huh?" Gode

asked. "That not enough to peak the int'rest o' the big bad Detective?"

Key pressed a fist against the desk, splitting the wood. He hoped that humoring Gode would move things along.

"What companies?" he asked, more focused on where that might lead him than concern for their safety. "Who was handing out faulty equipment?"

"Not sure," Gode said. "But it wasn't the equipment that was the issue."

"What, then?"

"They was rejectin' the prosthetics."

"What's that go to do with me?" Key asked. "Some people miss their doses of Hipotrex and end up in the weeds, big deal. Why's there a target on my head?"

"I didn't ask," Gode replied, grinning.

Key wanted to knock the man's teeth in. Gode knew full-well how furious he would get — Gode obviously *wanted* Key enraged. Even knowing this, Key couldn't help it. The rage flared and his hand moved — almost without his even thinking about it.

CHIBI STOOD, staring, as Key gripped Gode by the throat. Gode's hands raised in surrender.

"I didn't ask, but I still got a lead fo' ya," he choked out.

"Stop leading me on!"

Key slugged Gode in the face. "You're a worthless animal —"

Another punch.

"— that hides in his hole —"

Another.

"— and should have rotted in your mother's fucking belly!"

A final, bone-breaking punch sent Gode reeling and stumbling into his chair.

"What. Is. My. Name," Key demanded.

"I was gonna tell ya," he gasped, "but that's too bad . . . ya blew ya chance."

Gode whistled. There was a deafening *BANG*. A piercing shriek ripped through the air. Key's head snapped forward, blood blossoming from the back of his skull. He fell, dead, as Gode grinned. Fight or flight took full effect. Six went to draw her weapon and Chibi hit the ground. Another *BANG* and whistle, and Six had taken a bullet through the shoulder, dropping her gun. Chibi knew the shots were coming from outside the office, but he couldn't see the shooter.

"Ya good, boys!" Gode called, whistling again.

He turned his attention to Chibi and Six. His shit-eating grin was gone, replaced by a cold, blank stare. Chibi stared at Key's lifeless body. The dread set in as he knew the fight was over; there wasn't really a fight to begin with.

"Get the fuck outta my office," Gode commanded.

Without a second thought, Chibi grabbed the wounded Six and fled the office, rushing down the hall. His heart sank as he looked back at Key's body, lying in a pool of blood.

"You fucker!!" Six screamed, kicking and thrashing as Chibi struggled to drag her away, "I'll kill you!! You piece of *shit! I'LL TEAR YOUR FUCKING HEAD OFF!!"*

"Just business!" Gode called.

Chibi struggled, his breath labored. He walked past a few guys wearing the same colors as those they saw in the tunnel. It seemed Gode was right; word did travel fast in the Underground.

What a day . . . Chibi thought. *Oh, what a day . . .*

CHAPTER 17
FINALLY, HE HAD PEACE

Key opened his eyes. The last thing he remembered was looking at Gode's goblin-fucking face. He felt a dull pain at the back of his head, but his hand came away clean when he touched it. He looked around. He was sitting in a nice leather chair in some kind of lounge. The walls were a dark red and accented in mahogany. The room smelled like tobacco and the faint sound of jazz floated in the air. The entire scene felt incredibly familiar to Key, though he couldn't place it at all.

"Welcome."

Key leaped to his feet. He'd been sure he was alone, but a man stood behind the bar. The bartender smiled as Key cautiously walked towards him. With a half-nod, the bartender pulled out a bottle of what looked to be North Galivarian Whiskey, pouring two glasses. Key took a seat at the bar, snatching the nearer glass and sipping it. After a long silence, Key spoke.

"What do you mean 'welcome'?" he asked. "Where is this?"

"It could go by a few names," the bartender said, "but none of them truly do it justice."

Key gulped the rest of his whiskey, his throat burning as he set the glass down.

"Have I been here before?"

"Twice," the bartender replied. "Once before you became 'Key' and again after Med-Sec found you at Supe Ups."

"Then why don't I remember this place?" Key asked. "I mean it's familiar, but if I was just here a week ago, then I should actually *remember* it, right?"

"No, sir," the bartender answered. "You are made to forget each time you leave."

"I had enough of this around-the-bush crap with Gode," he said. "Give me answers or —"

He stopped short. His knife was gone. So was his gun.

"Where's my stuff?"

It was then that he looked at his attire. Gone were his jacket and pants, yukata-style shirt and sneakers. In their place, he wore a collared white shirt with the sleeves rolled up, navy waistcoat, tan pants, and a pair of gray and black cloth dress shoes. More shockingly, his hands were flesh. He realized his vision was normal — human. His eyes weren't bionic; there was no feed from the uplink in his head.

What the hell . . .? he thought.

"What the hell, indeed," the bartender said.

Key jumped from his seat, shuffling backwards until he hit a plush leather sofa.

"Did you just . . .?"

"Read your mind?"

The bartender's lips didn't move, but Key heard him clear as day. Afraid for the first time in a while, Key nodded.

"No," the bartender answered, mouth moving again. "At least not really."

"Then . . . what?"

"This is all your mind," the bartender replied. "The room, the smells, the sounds, the whiskey you drank, and even me, are all creations of your mind."

"How . . .?"

"In truth, I barely know more than you," the bartender

admitted. "Save the nature of this place, and the fact that you are dead, the only things I know are already dwelling within your mind."

That single word hit Key like a ton of bricks.

"Dead?"

"Yes, sir," the bartender answered. "You are dead."

"Then —"

"I believe it would be simpler if you didn't ask questions," the bartender said. "As I said, all that I know is already within your mind. However, there are many things you once knew that are now locked away. I alone hold the ability to reveal those to you again."

The wheels turned. Could it be true? Did the bartender know about Key's past?

"Yes, sir," the bartender said, answering the question Key had yet to ask. "I am the lock and you are the key." He smirked at the pun. "The only thing keeping you from remembering everything is your own will to forget — a service I am obliged to do for you, until such time as you relieve me of the duty."

Key thought hard, trying to piece together what the *hell* was going on. If he was dead, was this Heaven or something? Science had long since proven the energetic existence of the spirit or the soul or whatever, but they said that it all came and went through the Akashic. Was he in that great field of living energy — of mortal will and thought?

"Do you wish to remember?"

Key was pulled back from the spiral of thoughts. "What?"

"Do you wish for me to open the door, granting you the memories you have sealed away?"

Key would have thought the answer was clear; he'd spent three years trying to uncover his past. Yet, when faced with the apparent opportunity to regain what was lost, he was overcome with trepidation.

"I know that you are torn," the bartender said, voice caring. "Perhaps a small glimpse will help make your decision easier?"

Solemnly, Key nodded.

"Very well."

The bartender leaned forward as Key approached. He placed his fingers on Key's head, two on his temple, two behind his ear, and thumb under his eye.

"I hope you are satisfied."

In an instant, Key was somewhere else: a fancy bathroom, tiled in black marble. Unlike every time before, this was not a dream, distorted by his unconscious mind. He was remembering!

Holy hell . . .

He looked in the mirror but didn't recognize his face. On the one hand, he knew this would be the case — he was aware of the reconstruction Six had done — but it was no less alienating to see a man he didn't know reflected back at him; actually, he thought he looked quite a lot like the bartender. Perhaps worse, he was a passenger in his own body, along for the ride as his previous self carried on.

Splashing water on his face, he exited the bathroom, coming into a tacky bedroom. It was carpeted in red, with a large black-sheeted bed in the middle. Two lamps cast the room in a hazy, sultry light. Much to Key's surprise, there was a woman waiting on the bed, not a stitch of clothing on her. He didn't know her, but there was a vague sense of recognition. This woman was important to Key, once. She was beautiful, her wavy, blonde hair falling all about her face and on her chest, her body slender yet curvy, her stomach flat, but hips and chest ample. Key was attracted to say the least, feeling a pang of guilt as he thought about Six.

It's the past, he thought.

Key climbed into the bed, disrobing with some help from his partner, as the two kissed passionately.

In a blink, Key was whisked away from that scene, finding

himself standing at a very large window, high up and staring out at the city. He was alone, and he got the distinct feeling that something big was about to happen. He couldn't remember what, but he knew that it was going to happen tomorrow. Everything would be different tomorrow.

Again, the scene ended, landing Key in another memory. He couldn't see, but he could feel intense, excruciating pain. Every muscle in his body seized as he thrashed and screamed.

"Restrain him!" a voice yelled.

He felt a jolt that turned his every thought to a white void. Then dark. He felt the jolt again. Then dark. A third time, he felt the jolt. There was a split second where he could see. His writhing in agony caused him to roll, revealing that he was lying on an operating table, wires and tubes sticking out of him. Two figures stood above him, though he couldn't tell who they were. Beyond the fact that he had no idea where he was or what was happening, they were wearing surgical masks and there was a spotlight in his face, turning them into fuzzy shadows.

"FUCKSHITDAMNFUCK!!"

Every single nerve in his body was a raging inferno. His blood was like acid and his mind couldn't even formulate enough of a thought to articulate pain. He longed to go back to the dark. He wanted to fall asleep again, maybe forever.

"I DON'T WANNA DIE!!!"

It was the only thought he could muster. There were no metathoughts, no remarks on his relived memories. All he had was the past, consuming his mind with pain. Though he knew death would mean the pain stopped, he didn't want it.

After a full two minutes of agony, his pain subsided.

I'm dead . . . he thought, cheering weakly.

Finally, he had peace.

KEY FELT like he was falling and snapped back to his quasi-reality in the bar. He pulled away from the bartender's touch, his fingers and toes still tingling. He looked at the bartender, pain, fear, regret, and anger swirling in his mind, each overtaking the other in rapid succession. He struggled to process what he'd seen. He drew a deep but ragged breath.

"What was that?" he asked.

"That was your past," the bartender replied. "Fragments of it, at least."

"But I . . . I died," Key said, still in disbelief.

"Yes, sir," the bartender affirmed. "As you have died now."

"Wha — h—how?!"

"I don't know, sir," the bartender admitted. "But during your first death, the trauma was too much. As a part of your resurrection, I locked away the past for your protection. Then you returned to life again."

"Will I come back this time?"

"I assure you that you will," the bartender said. "That is the purpose of this room: a place for your mind to wait until your body is ready."

The jazz reached a trumpet-heavy crescendo as Key's thoughts fell silent. The song ended, leaving his head empty — devoid of thought and sensation.

I have to get out of here.

Gripped by fear and still reeling from the taste of his past, he got up, breaking into a stride somewhere between a walk and a jog for a door on the far wall.

"Sir, you can't leave yet!" the bartender called. "The process isn't finished!"

Key didn't listen, grabbing the knob and throwing the door open. Everything beyond was a black and all-encompassing room of void and nothingness. Was that his afterlife or something else? He took a step forward. No sooner had his foot crossed the threshold, he felt a tug like someone had grabbed him by the shirt, his very essence being dragged away to somewhere else. He tried to turn — to flee — fearing this was the hand of Thanatos at his heart. His vision narrowed, and he felt like he was falling into a hole, or perhaps going backwards into a tunnel. Key looked to the bartender who simply smiled and waved.

"I'll keep the place clean!" he called, far-off and echoing.

The bar slipped from Key's vision, replaced by nothing but darkness.

CHAPTER 18
NO THOUGHTS, ONLY IMPULSES

Chibi and Six rode silently. It had been a long time since Chibi had to paddle a boat — must have been when he went on a field trip in high school — but there was no way Six was going to do it.

She hadn't spoken since they left Gode. The whole way back to the canal, into the raft, and for the ride so far, she'd been completely silent. Chibi tried his best to use the time to his advantage. He was sure Key would have been able to do better, but this wasn't the time for futile comparisons. Key was gone.

Think! Chibi mentally shouted at himself. *What do you know . . .?*

He thought back to everything, going as far as weeks back. He tried to piece together what little he knew with what Gode had said. He was surely no Detective, but he was there. Whatever fell chance of circumstance had led him there, he decided to try.

People disappearin' after they sta'ted havin' issues wit they bionics . . . They was rejectin' the prosthetics.

I knew about this, Chibi thought. *At work, people had started calling in about their prosthetics acting up — way more than usual —*

and a bunch said their body was trying to . . . "push out" the arm or something like that . . .

He remembered the man in black who broke into his apartment. The one he'd killed. How the guy had taunted him.

I wasn't even there for the train crash — just supposed to search your place for damning evidence. I guess we got the wrong guy, though . . . It's not about some little salary slave . . . this is big shit — top of the food chain shit.

Chibi ran a hand through his hair, puzzled. *They thought I was connected to this somehow, but why? I just got caught in the crossfire.*

He decided to take a momentary break from sleuthing to try and check in on Six. He didn't know how to start.

"Six . . .?"

"They killed him . . ." she murmured. "They . . ." — sniff — "they fucking killed him . . ."

He may have only known Key for a few days, but Chibi still felt the loss. Less crushing, more a nagging ache and a shadow over his countenance, he felt the death of Key.

"I'm sorry," Chibi said quietly. "If I hadn't killed that jackboot back at my place, maybe —"

"Stop," Six said, voice cold and level. "He didn't die because of you. He died chasing himself. There's nothing to apologize for."

"But Six, I —"

"This is just how he was," Six interrupted. "He's never really been able to accept the loss of his past. I tried to help, but I'm no good with investigations or any of that."

Six sniffed. Chibi decided not to speak.

"Enoch was at least able to give him purpose by making him a Black Angel and setting him up as a Detective," she said, barely holding back her tears. "He needed so badly to know who he was, he didn't care where the lead was coming from."

Chibi wracked his brain for something — anything — to say. Something to keep her from breaking.

"He was a gangster," Chibi said. "This was bound to happen eventually."

Chibi was at the front of the raft, facing forward, but he could sense danger behind him. He stopped paddling, turning to see a gun barrel in his face.

"Fucking say that again," Six said, sadness replaced with a cold, focused rage.

Chibi's hands went up, silently begging for mercy.

"I — I —" he stammered.

"Fucking. Say it. Again."

"This . . ." Chibi started, trying desperately to discern what to do, "was bound to happen?"

Six shot to her feet, still pointing her gun in Chibi's face.

"He deserved it!?" she screamed, tears undercutting her rage, as her voice echoed in the dark tunnel. "Key fucking *deserved* to die!?"

Her return to despair didn't make her any less threatening, Chibi still holding up his hands in surrender.

"I didn't say that," he corrected. "I just —"

"No, no, I get it," Six said. "It's because he was a Sundowner, right?"

Chibi was terrified to answer.

"That's all we Sundowners are good for, right?" she demanded. "Just because you got some new clothes and a haircut doesn't change you."

Chibi figured it was well-deserved after all he had said since stumbling into their lives, but that didn't take the sting out. The two stared at each other, Six's face turning red as she collapsed back into the raft. She dropped the gun, clutching her wounded shoulder as she wept. Chibi considered comforting her, but decided he'd done enough damage.

He resumed paddling.

KEY OPENED HIS EYES. He had no thoughts, only impulses.

He sat straight up, the metal floor he was laying on barely registering in his mind. A couple of people in white bomber jackets and red, long-nosed masks rushed towards him in the cramped space that was the back of a vehicle, but he paid them little mind. A swipe of the hand and a punch caved their skulls well enough. He didn't have time to worry about people getting in his way. He was in a van — maybe a truck — but it didn't matter. He kicked the door open and jumped out. He heard the vehicle screech and turn, but he didn't care. He just started running. He ran and ran, not sure where he was going — certainly not taking the time or energy to think about it — but he continued all the same, running for block after block on bare feet.

He had no thoughts, only impulses.

Arriving at what seemed to be the place his unconscious mind was driving him toward, he came to a halt in the middle of a busy, blocked-off street. The glow from an alley beckoned, the neon rainbow singing like a siren's song. Slowly, almost lumbering, he made his way into the alley, walking to the door at the end. No one stood in his way; in fact, he was welcomed.

Making his way to a booth inside, he took a seat. His head was filled with swirling sensations. He felt phantom pains like static electricity. He was numb. He was cold. He was tormented. He burned. Anything he tried to pull into his brain was drowned out by the cacophony. He squeezed his eyes shut, trying desperately to think. It didn't matter what it was, he just had to formulate a thought. *Something* to bring him out of the mire.

Two girls sat next to him, one on either side. They grabbed him by the arms and dragged him back to reality.

"Hey there," one of them purred. "Haven't seen you around."

She had cat ears on her head and blue patterns painted on her face.

"Definitely not," the other cooed, batting her feathered

eyelashes. "I'd remember if my eyes feasted on a delicious snack like you."

"I can let you have a taste," Cat-girl whispered, putting Key's hand on her thigh.

"I'm the one who tastes."

Key felt a tickle on his ear as Feather-lashes licked his neck. Cat-girl moved his hand higher. Key's heart raced. He had no thoughts, only impulses.

"Ooooo . . ." Cat-girl murmured. "You've got mods . . ."

"Metal is such a turn-on."

Feather-lashes took a deep breath and gripped his chest. Cat-girl ran out of leg, grabbing her breast in one hand and running the other up and down Key's arm. Feather-lashes started to kiss his neck, fondling his chest. She pressed against him as Cat-girl put his hand between her legs. Both started to moan softly. Feather-lashes moved his collar, kissing lower on his neck. Lower. She reached his nape, flicking her tongue over his skin. She slid her hand up the back of his shirt, running her finger over his spine.

"We're going to do wonderful things to you."

Key heard her but didn't hear *her*. He couldn't place the voice, but it made his head spin. He slumped onto Cat-girl, now more or less at her climax as his mind slipped away. The lights narrowed into a neon-haze. For a moment, he thought he'd been drugged, but that slipped away, too. All he could sense was the touch on his spine as Feather-lashes whispered in his ear.

"We're going to do wonderful things to you."

The voice morphed and distorted. Key's heart pounded in his chest as blood rushed in his ears. He could feel light strobing on his face as he rolled down a hallway. He couldn't move but he felt the dread.

"We're going to do wonderful things to you."

Feather-lashes dug her nails into his back. Life flashed back into Key as his muscles surged with adrenaline. Metal and flesh alike flew to action, lifting Key and Feather-lashes from the bench. Like the van, his body was moving on instinct.

No thoughts, only impulses.

His hand clenched. He could hear Feather-lashes whimpering as Cat-girl pleaded in fear, but Key wasn't the one at the wheel.

No thoughts, only impulses.

Every eye was on him. A dozen guns, too.

"Put her down!" Cat-girl screamed.

The bar patrons opened fire, the bullets ripping through flesh and bouncing off metal. For the second time, Key felt his life slipping away. He released Feather-lashes, dropping her to the floor as he followed suit. As he lay on the floor, blood pooling around him, he was afraid. He couldn't understand what came over him — what compelled him. Who was the voice he heard?

"We're going to do wonderful things to you."

He had no thoughts, only pain.

CHAPTER 19
SOMETHING OF HIS PAST

Key awakened, once again in the dark, red bar. Rather than jazz, this time it was a soft piano number you might hear at a restaurant in one of the chic parts of town — the upper-east of the city. Still, the rest of the bar was unchanged. The bartender stood in the same place Key had left him.

"I told you not to leave yet, but I did as I promised and kept the place clean," the bartender said, not looking up from wiping the counter. "Still, I hadn't expected you to return so soon."

Key rose from his chair and walked over to the bar.

"Were you so eager for more of your past?" the bartender asked.

Key almost vomited, flashing back to the acid blood and fire skin.

"No," he replied, "I'm not even sure what the hell happened."

"Well," the bartender started, pouring two glasses of the same whiskey, "it appears you had what you might call a 'rebooting error', sir. I imagine that's also the reason you remember this place now."

"I'm not a damn computer."

"How not?" the bartender asked. "At this point, you're as much metal as man, not to mention that your entire being runs off of electrical impulses — biological ones and zeroes, compartmentalized in a fleshy hard drive. You've even gone as far as to create a half-conscious subroutine to sandbox your memories, so tell me again how you're not a computer?"

Key sipped his whiskey.

"I confess that I don't understand it fully," the bartender admitted, "but I'd deduce that you seized control of your body before higher functions were restored and the deep freeze protocol could remove the memory of the Red Room."

"Meaning?"

"Your unbridled Id led you to a familiar place, but, with no impulse control, you swiftly got yourself killed. Additionally, I am no longer able to cause you to forget the things that occur while you are here," the bartender answered. "I assure you that I won't allow the same mistake."

"How can you guarantee that?"

The bartender snapped and all the doors in the room vanished.

"For your own good."

Key squirmed a little. While the bartender did have a point, he'd often struggled with seeing himself as less than human. Being confronted with it, even if only as a logical analogy, was . . . uncomfortable. With no past, half a body, and no family —

No, he thought. *I had a family.*

Six. She'd always tried to get him to look past what once was and accept what he had in the present. He thought about the day they got married. It was a small affair, strictly for them and their friends to have a few drinks and a good time. She wore a yellow dress, and he a blue suit. They exchanged rings and swore oaths to always be together; they swore to love each other always.

"She was quite beautiful at the wedding, sir."

Key was shaken. Not only was he lost in thought, but having his mind read was still less than desirable.

"Can I get drunk in here?" Key asked.

"What do you mean, sir?"

"Well, this isn't real, right?" — he gestured to the room and his glass — "It's all a construct of my mind."

"Correct."

"You're not real. My body isn't real. It's all just sensory information to keep my conscious mind occupied so I don't have to deal with the trauma of coming back to life, right?"

"Yes."

"So I can't get drunk."

"I didn't say that."

The bartender snapped and the world started to spin. Key felt a bit like he was floating, his arms heavy and vision blurred. He tried to take a drink of his whiskey but ended up sloshing it onto the bar. Another snap and all was back to normal.

"As you said, sir," the bartender whispered, "this is *your* world."

SIX AND CHIBI floated into the station where they had begun their journey, albeit one member short. Chibi disembarked, extending a hand to Six to help her out. She groaned in pain, still clutching her shoulder, but ignored his offer. As Chibi pulled the raft up onto the platform, dragging it to where the others sat, Six walked up the stairs without him. They emerged back into the world of rain, turning into the alley, now alive with activity. Before they even got to Kanpai, Chibi could hear the music. Before they entered, he could smell the smoke and booze. As soon as they'd gotten through the door, Enoch grabbed them both by the arms and whisked them through the crowd to his office.

"*Suwaru.*"

With the door closed, the party faded to a dull beat and the faint whiff of excess.

"What do you want?" Six asked, tone flat.

"Key . . ." Enoch started, face betraying his pain, "he's flatlined."

"We know," Chibi said. "We were there."

Enoch paused a moment, face shifting from distraught to confused.

"*Ie*," Enoch replied. "*Yakusoku* you weren't."

"I think I'd remember watching him die," Six spat. "We were there."

"*Bakane*." Enoch said. "He flatlined in the bar."

FOR SOME REASON, it was easy for Key to believe he could come back from the dead. Truthfully, it was the only explanation he had for why he was alive in the first place. Six, Doc, and basically every medical journal said he should never have survived the damage that was done to his body three years prior. Blood loss alone should have killed him, not to mention the shock, organ damage, and brain hemorrhaging. Any one of those could have put him in the obituaries, and yet he was alive.

Before they even found him — when he was just the writhing remains of a battered torso, head, and a single leg — he was alive. Who knows how long he was in the bio-dump before they found him? Resurrection was as valid an explanation as any other he could think of. Definitely explained how he stood up unharmed from a fire he was in the dead middle of.

"Tell me about the old me," he said, sitting at the bar and sipping his whiskey. "Am I actually the Heihachi Hanamura Med-Sec seems to think I am?"

"I could just —"

"No," Key said, batting away the bartender's extended hand, "I can't handle remembering like that."

"Very well," the bartender capitulated. "What would you like to know?"

"Who was the woman?"

"Sir?"

"The blonde woman in my memory," Key clarified. "Who was she? To me, I mean."

"That would have been your first life partner, Lillian Matthew," the bartender answered. "She was a Terran immigrant you met while working for . . . a technologies firm."

Key was curious. Who had he worked for? How did he end up with a Terran immigrant for a wife?

"She was never your wife," the bartender said. "She didn't believe in marriage and neither did you."

Key took a long sip from his glass, setting it on the bar in front of him. Flashes of conversations sparked in his mind. Painful arguments. Insults. Lies.

"You gotta stop reading my mind," he said. "Freaks me out."

"I am your mind."

Key took a deep breath, letting it out in a sigh.

"Just . . . wait for me to talk out loud, okay?"

"Understood."

Key stared into the whiskey. He'd been drinking consistently, but his glass never got any emptier. He thought about the little chunks of memory he'd regained. He thought about the bedroom and Lilly. He thought about the window and the promise of "tomorrow." He remembered the pain. Blood like acid, skin like fire. But he'd regained another memory, too. When he was in the club — when Id was running the show — he'd remembered something else.

We're going to do wonderful things to you . . .

What did it mean? Whatever it was, it had sent him into a spiral that had him choking a girl. It made him feel dizzy and distant, like he was being drugged. Was that part of the memory?

"Does the phrase 'we're going to do wonderful things to you' mean anything?" Key asked the bartender. "I heard it when I was out of control, and it sent me for a *ride*."

"I'm not at liberty to say."

"I'm giving you liberty."

The bartender sighed, pulling out a rag to start wiping glasses.

"It's what the doctors said to you as they put you under for your tortures."

Key puzzled over this. "Why would that be traumatizing?"

"You knew the full extent of what awaited you," the bartender said. "You were betrayed, but too drugged up to do anything about it."

A thought began to blossom in Key's mind. Like a word on the tip of his tongue, there was a memory trying desperately to get out but unable to break through.

"You thought you were going to pioneer the future, but that was not your fate," the bartender continued. "You had become fodder for richer men."

The bar faded slightly, as the piano turned to a droning. Key's movements slowed and the bartender's words slurred. He began to remember.

Prometheus Suprema. That was the program.

He remembered the promise of a bright future. He was supposed to be on the forefront; he was to be in the spearhead that launched military technology — hell, the mortal form — into the next level.

"You were proud," the bartender said, Key still able to clearly make out his words, "but it all fell apart."

Key's head started to ache. It went from a dull throb to a full-blown migraine in seconds, turning his stupor to a complete haze.

"I was a subject in the Prometheus Suprema program?"

"Eventually," the bartender answered. "But you tried to take more than you should have. You betrayed them. Then, when they started the torture, you knew what you'd done. You knew what you gave up."

Key's head pounded as his mind was flooded with fragments of memory. Faces he couldn't recognize, names he didn't know, and places he couldn't recall all flooded through his mind. It was like a firehose being blasted at him, each shard of a memory coming so hard it left him reeling — too fast to process.

"Stop . . ." he groaned.

"They tore you apart to see if they could put you back together."

"Stop."

"Your fingers and toes, arms and legs, they ripped and tore just to build you back again."

"Stop!" Key roared.

"You asked to remember, sir," the bartender said flatly. "I'm only doing as I was told."

Key's pain slowly receded, leaving him panting. He downed the rest of his whiskey, but he couldn't drown his newfound thirst. His body ached. He let out a whimper.

"How could I forget all of that?" he asked, starting to cry. "How could that pain ever go away?"

"It didn't, sir," the bartender answered. "You just chose not to look at it."

Those words hung heavy in the air as Key tried to regain composure. So many memories and so much pain had come in like a tide, only to dissipate just as quickly. The whole thing left him dazed. Still, the bartender was right. It was like his mom had always said: Hiding the garbage didn't get rid of the smell.

Wait . . .

For a split second, Key had remembered his mother. He tried desperately to chase that memory, to pull a face or a voice from the black abyss of his past, but he came up empty.

"My mom!" he shouted. "I remembered her, just now!"

"You loved your parents dearly," the bartender said. "I'm not surprised that one of them resurfaced."

"She's gone, though . . ." Key wailed. "I had it for a moment, but I can't draw her out again."

He felt a deep hole in his chest. Remembering Lilly was one thing, but this fleeting memory of his mother had taken something with it. Or, perhaps, reminded him of what was already missing.

Bing.

A soft chime sounded overhead.

"I'm sorry, sir, but your body is ready," the bartender said. "I haven't the time to help you grab ahold of your past again."

"I can stay!" Key said, a little frantic. "I want to remember more!"

"You can't, sir," the bartender said, morose. "Just as it was a mistake for you to return to your body too early, I cannot hold you indefinitely."

"Please," Key begged, "please help me remember."

The world started to go dark. Key could feel life pulling him.

"You *are* Heihachi Hanamura," the bartender said, voice drifting. "Find that name and you will find the truth of who you are. That name will lead you to the answers you aren't ready to remember."

His voice got further and further away.

"And, please, sir, don't return anytime soon."

"He got plugged by some squibs during some monkey shit," Enoch said. "I have his body."

Chibi sat in stunned silence. He didn't imagine Enoch was lying, but how could he be telling the truth? He and Six had watched with their own eyes as Key was shot by Tengu's guys. How could he have possibly been killed at Kanpai?

"Don't toy with me, Enoch!" Six screamed. "I had to leave him in the Underground! Don't tell me you have him when you couldn't!"

Enoch pushed a button on his desk. The door opened behind them. A large man with what might as well have been a robot gorilla's arms came in, a large black bag in tow.

"Never, *okini,*" Enoch said solemnly. "Couldn't even have dreams of it."

The gorilla man set the bag on the couch on the far right of the office, unzipping it to reveal Key's body. Six clapped her hands over her mouth as her sobbing started all over again. She leaped from her chair, throwing her arms around the corpse of her fallen husband. She wailed into his chest, soaking his shirt with her tears. Chibi slowly rose from his chair, looking for himself, as the gorilla man exited the room.

"Told you I wasn't spittin' lies," Enoch said.

"We can see that," Chibi said. "But it doesn't make sense."

"We have to give him a burial," Six whispered, sniffing and sobbing. "I don't know how you got him, but I won't let anyone touch his body."

She stood, wiping her cheeks and nose.

"How would he have wanted it?" Chibi asked. "Ashes in the sea? Planted with a cherry tree growing from his chest?"

Six cracked a smile. It was a deeply sad smile, but one rooted in a joy that had yet to be extinguished. She laughed a little.

"He always wanted us to launch his body into the sun," she said. "He said it was the only way he'd ever get to see it."

"I guess we could —"

Chibi didn't finish his sentence. All three of them froze as they heard a rustling come from the body bag. Slowly, they all turned to face the bag, sadness supplanted by terror. When Key sat up, they lost their shit.

"AAAAAAAAGH!!!" Chibi screamed.

Six jumped out of her skin, literally leaping backwards as she shrieked.

"Whathefuck whathefuck whatheFUCK!!"

Enoch slid his chair away, eyes wide and mouth agape. He was completely frozen, unable to even scream as he stared at the reanimated, blood-soaked form of his friend.

"Where am I?" Key asked sleepily.

A new wave of shock and horror washed over the others as

they screamed again. Gorilla arms must have heard them, because he came in, followed closely by another thuggish-looking guy. They, too, screamed when they saw Key sitting up out of the body bag, slamming the door and running away.

"Stop screaming!" Key complained. "My head is killing me."

"That would be the bullet!" Chibi yelled. "Why are you talking!?"

"Stop. Screaming," Key repeated, wincing.

After a few slow, deep breaths, everyone seemed to calm down. They were confused, overwhelmed, and probably still a bit afraid, but they weren't hyperventilating anymore.

"H-ho-how . . .?" Six asked breathlessly. "How are you alive . . .?"

"Are you sure that I died?" Key asked.

"Yes!!" Enoch cried, "No doubt in our brain you died!"

"I don't think it's the first time," Key said. "The bartender said this was the fourth time I died."

"The who?" Chibi asked.

"The —" Key broke off. "It doesn't matter right now."

He climbed out of the body bag, sitting on the couch next to it.

They really did think I was dead. I guess they weren't wrong, though.

The other three stared at him, causing a shiver to go down his spine. He felt . . . off. He'd have to confess that it was weird. He'd died twice that day, and yet he sat on the couch thinking about nothing but how badly he wanted a cheeseburger steak. Then his mind drifted to the wider things — the memories he'd recovered. He tried to keep the nausea at bay.

"I remembered some things," he said.

Enoch and Six's eyes were wide, and a slight gasp escaped Six's lips.

"I remembered that I actually did volunteer for an experiment," he continued. "Something about becoming a super soldier, but . . ."

The pain and sickness started to swell. He decided to shy away from going further.

"I didn't."

He could see the gears spinning a-mile-a-minute in their heads. It kind of felt good to be able to tell them some things; finally, he had something of his past to share.

"I remembered that I actually . . . had . . . a life partner before," he said, somewhat sheepishly.

Six cocked an eyebrow.

"Oh?"

Key immediately regretted sharing that.

"I also remembered my name."

Kind of remembered it.

Everyone went deathly silent. Key smiled.

"Heihachi Hanamura."

CHAPTER 20
NO INTENTION OF LEAVING

The shock of Key coming back to life was wearing off. Their sorrow had barely had time to process, so it didn't take too long for them to readjust. The shock that he *could* was not fading so quickly. Nor was the fact that he had finally, after three years, recovered some memories; at least that's what Chibi came to understand as he looked at Enoch and Six's awed stares.

"As it turns out, I asked my brain to forget my past," Key said.

"You did what?" Chibi asked. "How do you even *ask* your brain to do something?"

"I don't know," Key replied, groaning and putting his head in his hands. "There's a lot of weird going on here, and I don't get it."

"You're alive," Six said. "That's the part we need to focus on."

She sat next to Key, placing a hand on his shoulder as she kissed his cheek.

"Let's go home," she said. "You look tired."

"That idea is shit," Enoch said, shaking his head. "You guys need to dig a hole and hide where no one's gonna plug him in the dome again."

"He's my husband and I'm taking him home," Six said, voice quiet but commanding. "Stand in my way and I guarantee you'll live to regret it."

Enoch folded his hands, but he simply nodded. Six helped Key to his feet and walked out of the office, Chibi close behind.

Outside the office, the party raged on. One would never guess that a man had been shot five times on that very dance floor. Perhaps Chibi had had a point when he threw shade at the frequent deaths in the Cauldron. Regardless, the bar showed no signs of altercation. Six weaved Key through the crowd, leading him past those who had killed him just hours prior. None took notice.

BACK AT THEIR APARTMENT, Six led Key to the bedroom. He tore off his tattered clothes, throwing them against the wall rather than the laundry. Six handed him some fresh ones, pulling back the covers to put him in bed. He settled into the jersey sheets and double pillows, already feeling himself slip towards unconsciousness. Resurrection took a lot out of him.

"I love you, Six," he said.

She crawled into the bed next to him, laying her head on his chest.

"I love you, too," she murmured. "I'm never letting you go again."

Key stared at the ceiling. He blinked, the ceiling shifting — for the briefest of moments — to one painted white. Another blink turned it back to dull gray, but that image resonated in his mind. Like a shout into a valley, the white ceiling echoed back. It brought no images or strings of memories, only the vague sense of comfort and familiarity one feels at home. Whether it was being at home that triggered it or the memory that brought the feeling, it was utterly mundane, yet so profound.

"I have no intention of leaving," he said, slipping off to sleep.

CHIBI SAT ON THE COUCH, now alone in the apartment. Just over a week ago, he'd been dragged through the front door and laid in the same spot he now sat. At that point, he thought it would still be possible to go back to normal. He was wrong. Then again, what did he even want to go back to? He'd been grinding away at Kigen for years but never went anywhere. He never talked to anyone at work, he lost touch with all his college friends, and he barely spoke to his family. What so alluring about "normal"?

Moot point, now . . .

The moment he'd gotten out of his seat on the train was the moment his fate was sealed. However, that fact was finally starting to settle on him. He was working with Enoch, he had a roof over his head and people who were starting to open up to him; he was gaining their trust.

CHAPTER 21
AN EQUAL PART OF THE TEAM

After waking from his sleep, Key felt a renewed sense of vigor and purpose. He had a goal, but, more importantly, he had a lead.

Heihachi Hanamura, he thought. *Who are you?*

He'd been rudderless the past three years. It was sheer desperation that drove him to Med-Sec. He knew they were a nest of hornets and vipers, but he didn't know where else to go. He surely didn't expect to become the target of a manhunt, but he was foolish to think it would go off without consequences. Now, he actually had hope that he might uncover something. He knew his name at least, but there's a world of difference between a name and a man. He needed to know *who* he was.

It's time.

He strode out of his room, closing the door and leaving Six to finish dressing for the day. Chibi and Ajax were sitting on the couch. They both sat in silence, looking everywhere but Key's direction. He realized he'd made things a bit awkward for them the last time they were there. He chose to ignore it.

"Chibi," he said, taking a seat on the coffee table. "I know you used to work for Kigen. Do you reckon you could still get in the building?"

Chibi met his eyes, face painted with fear.

"I thought I had to lay low," he said. "You said I was 'burned' and 'have no life anymore' and all that."

"I didn't say you'd be walking in the front door like nothing happened," Key said.

"Then . . .?"

"Spy shit," Ajax interjected. "Key wants you to use your credentials to get in the building, get whatever it is we're after, and get out before Med-Sec responds to shoot your ass."

Key broke eye contact.

"Is that right?" Chibi demanded. "Are you seriously asking me to do that?"

"That's assuming it isn't Kigen that wants me, and — by extension, you — killed."

"What!?" Chibi exclaimed, jumping to his feet. "What the hell makes you think that!?"

"Well," Key started, a little sheepish, "three reasons. First, the speed with which they thought you might be involved suggests a deeper connection between you and I than we are aware of. Second, Kigen and Med-Sec have always been tight, so it makes sense that this level of firepower would get called in if it really is them pulling the strings."

Key paused, causing Chibi to squirm.

"What's number three?"

"Enoch got back to us about the biotech we pulled from the Med-Sec guys," Key answered. "Not only are all of the pieces Kigen, but they were all registered to former Kigen employees."

"So you want me to walk into what you believe is the one place where everyone who wants me dead is currently standing?" Chibi asked, incredulous.

"We'll back you up," Key assured him, "but . . . yeah, kinda."

Chibi collapsed to the couch, head in his hands.

"Why the hell did you save my life if you were just going to throw me to the wolves?"

"He's not throwing you to the wolves," Six said, joining the conversation. "Very much the opposite."

"How?" Chibi asked, panic clearly starting to set in. "How is this *not* sending me to die?"

"One," Key said, holding up a finger. "I'm not going to let you die. Two," — another finger — "I'm not sending you off on your own. I'm asking you to join the team."

Chibi ran his shaking hands through his hair. He sat back and beat his chest, giving a primal shout. He locked eyes with Key. Key could see a myriad of emotions — fear, mostly — but he saw the all-important spark in those eyes: determination.

THREE DAYS of planning and prep later, they were ready for their attack on Kigen.

"This is insane," Chibi said, standing outside Zaibatsu.

They had waited until late evening to launch their plan. All the regular personnel had left the building, only security and a few stragglers remaining. Chibi knew damn well he couldn't fake his way through this; he had basically zero people skills when he couldn't hide behind the phone, and he was too terrified to try. He just had to be unassuming. Draw as little attention to himself as possible. If the security team had no reason to approach him, there'd be no problems whatsoever. At least that's what he kept telling himself.

Stay calm, he thought. *Cool and collected. That's me. Cool. And. Collected.*

He'd traded the bright clothes he'd borrowed — and quickly come to love — for something less eye-grabbing. Key called it attention-whorish and Six scolded him, but Chibi genuinely didn't mind. If he didn't know better, he'd say they were actually developing a rapport. Now decked out once again in a drab gray suit with a knit hat to cover the plate on his head, he prayed for his old ways to carry him through. No one had ever talked to him before, so why would they start?

It's perfect, really, he thought, trying desperately to reassure himself.

"This is completely insane," he muttered, trying not to *look* insane as he talked to himself. "They will totally have shut off my badge if I'm actually burned."

In truth, he was not talking to himself; the rest of the team were listening in.

"You really think a company as massive and bureaucratic as Kigen deactivated your badge this quick?" Key asked in the earpiece, his voice as clear as if he were standing beside Chibi.

Key did have a point. Chibi once asked for a day off to go to his grandfather's funeral, and it took a week to get a response. Truth be told, HR probably hadn't even been told that they *should* deactivate his badge.

"Don't worry," Six assured him. "We're right here if anything happens."

"I wish you were *here,*" Chibi complained.

"You want a multiple-meter-tall machine-man and a dude who's got demon eyes to walk into Zaibatsu with you?" Ajax asked, only partially joking.

"I don't have demon eyes," Key said, sounding mildly offended.

"You think some rando working front desk security won't take one look at you and say 'that's a motherfuckin' demon!'?" Ajax asked.

"Shut up," Chibi growled. "I'm going in."

Clenching his fists, every fiber of his being screaming that he was making a mistake, Chibi steeled himself and entered Zaibatsu.

He knew the front door would be open — they never locked it, as the executives were known to keep odd hours — but he was still a bit surprised when it slid open on his approach. He did his best to remain inconspicuous, utilizing his umbrella to obscure his face. However, he had to close it eventually. As he did, the guard took notice.

"Sir!" he called across the vast lobby.

Keep. Calm. Nothing is wrong, Chibi assured himself.

He tapped his umbrella to shake off the rain and walked over to the guard's desk.

"After hours check-in," the guard said apologetically. "We just like to have a closer eye on who's coming and going."

"Shit."

Chibi meant it to be in his head, but it certainly wasn't.

"Sir?"

"Nothing," Chibi said, desperately trying to not let this slip away. "I have my badge right here."

He reached into his jacket and withdrew his badge. There was a pang of loss and regret as he looked at the picture on it. A youthful Shio Shimada stared back. A young man full of hope, not yet lost to self-pity and unmet expectations.

What a sack of shit I became . . .

"Sir?" the guard said, hand extended.

Chibi realized he'd been staring. He quickly handed over the badge. The guard took it, touching it to the scanner and looking to the screen. Chibi watched him intently. He seemed like a nice enough guy, but that was nothing to go on.

Might have to kill him . . .

Where did that thought come from?

"All good, Mister Shimada," the guard said, handing Chibi his badge.

Chibi took it, flashing a smile, and headed for the elevator. As the doors slid shut, he let out a deep sigh. He looked down at his hand, white-knuckled on his umbrella.

"I hate this," he whispered.

"We knew you could do it," Six said.

"Now's the easy part," Key chimed in. "You just have to go to the records room."

"Why, though?" Chibi asked. "Why do I have to *physically* walk into the room for this to work?"

"Because I can't get access via wireless connection," Ajax explained. "You plugging a wireless receiver into their servers will let me do that."

"Then why aren't you here!?" Chibi hissed, suppressing a shout.

"We just talked about this," Ajax said. "But I'll say it again. You want a two-meter —"

"No," Chibi interrupted, "I'd have a far worse time trying to explain you."

"Then stop complaining," Ajax chided. "We have no idea how long we have until you get discovered and they start after you."

"Don't worry, though," Six assured him, "We're monitoring broad-frequency communications."

Bing.

The elevator chimed and the doors slid open. Chibi emerged to the empty floor. It was eerie without the constant hustle and bustle of the day. Granted, this wasn't his floor, so he'd have felt out of place even if it was, but the stark quiet certainly didn't help. The lights came on, flickering to life in succession down the hall. The entirety of the floor was dedicated to the immense technological needs of Kigen's networks, phones, and data. Unfortunately for Chibi and the crew, they were smart enough to keep their sensitive data off the web. Patient information — "client data" if you asked anyone in the company — was kept with Med-Sec, while project files were kept right inside Kigen.

Can't trust anyone else with the trillion jul ideas.

That's what he was after. He needed to plug the receiver into the offline servers so Ajax could patch in and dig around. A perk of being a machine lifeform: he could integrate with computers using his brain and a WebLink. The downside: failure meant brain death. For an Oran, the brain was all they had — it was what they were. As Ajax explained it, body-hopping was easy.

All they had to do was take the motherboard from an Oran and stick it into a new body; but that also made them as vulnerable as any other machine.

Robots with souls, Chibi thought. *The Akashic truly did work wonders.*

He looked around at the towering servers, separated from him by thick glass walls. Their myriad blinking lights seemed to stare at him like a million eyes from the darkness. Exabytes of data all written in strands of qubits. Literal, solid bricks of data locked in quantum states until summoned. When he thought about it like that, technology and the supposed "Akashic Magicks" truly didn't seem so different. Especially since Chibi understood neither.

"What now?" he asked.

"Now you start plugging me into towers until we find what we're looking for," Ajax instructed. "Every line of towers will be linked in series, but you'll have to still move the receiver to a new line every time I don't find what we're after."

"And what are we after? You've given me the bones of the plan, but I don't know *why* we're doing this."

"Because, like I keep telling you, you don't need to know," Ajax said.

"I'm an equal part of the team, right?" Chibi asked. "That's what you said, Key."

"Chibi, you really don't —"

"Project Prometheus," Key interrupted. "We're currently looking for a name — that Heihachi guy — but the goal is Project Prometheus."

Chibi's heart genuinely warmed. He had felt a bit like an appendage, if not an inconvenience or outright hazard, but for the first time, he felt like he was actually their partner.

"Got it."

CHAPTER 22
TO BE IMMORTAL

Key sat with his hands folded, knees bouncing. He was worried. Had he entrusted too much to Chibi? He'd only known the guy a couple weeks, and here he was asking him to put his life on the line. That was . . . a lot. Key's fear slowly crept in.

Am I too hungry? he thought. *Was this a mistake?*

He may have opened a door when he went to Med-Sec, but that didn't save him from rushing into things. If he'd been more patient, they could have come up with a better plan, but here they were. He was going off half-cocked and wasn't even the one that would suffer the consequences.

"Are you finding it?" Key asked.

"No," Ajax replied. "I'm hitting the system with queries, but it's not turning anything up."

"How deep are you digging?"

"I'm scanning full text. *If* there's a file on Heihachi, we're going to find it."

Key went back to bouncing, holding his chin in his clasped hands.

"It's going to be fine," Six said, trying to be reassuring. "You know Ajax is doing his best."

"I do," Key admitted. "But I'm still worried."

He tried to come up with a contingency plan. What were they going to do when Med-Sec showed up? Chibi was on the 132nd floor. There's no way he'd be able to get down fast enough.

If only I thought about this longer . . . planned better.

They could fight. That was an option — but not a great one. Chibi could hide, but he had a Kigen ID on him, so they'd be able to track him. Even if he dumped it, these were Med-Sec jackboots; the boogeymen of Galivaria, dispatching squads of black-clad soldiers to clean up any leaks. Key was one such leak.

"I found a mention of Heihachi," Ajax said. "It's not much, but I can cross-reference now."

"What'd you find?!" Key asked excitedly.

"His name came up in a file regarding corporate succession rights."

"He's Kigen corporate?" Six asked, her tone betraying her surprise.

"SHH!" Ajax hushed. "I have to focus or we'll run out of time."

Key couldn't sit still. He tried crossing his legs, but they were still bouncing. He held them with his hands and his whole body shook. For the first time in three years, he was on the edge of learning something. Med-Sec may have been a last-ditch effort to try and discover something, but it paid off. It may have created a mess, and it certainly wasn't straightforward, but it was something. It was finally something.

CHIBI HAD GONE through five server rows before Ajax found anything. It's not like his job was hard, but the anticipation was killer — both of results and the all-important moment he'd have to flee. He plugged in the receiver for the sixth time. The indicator light came on and the machine whirred to life. He sat, hunkered against a wall to limit the amount he was visible as much as possible. No way there weren't cameras, but he did what he could. He listened to the conversation over the comm.

"I have to focus or we'll run out of time," Ajax scolded.

It wasn't much, but it was a lead. Heihachi might have been Kigen Corporate. It would certainly make enough sense. Rumors had been spreading for a couple years that Kigen was trying to reverse engineer the immortality tech of the Demigods. Chibi chose to ride that thought to carry him away from his stresses.

The Demigods were an elite group of Empyreans, so Chibi didn't know much about them. He knew they were immortal and were *super* rich, but he didn't know which came first. It was more or less the law of the land — worlds, really — that money could buy anything in the Union. Corporations owned entire planets, the executive staff ruling like royalty. With the dynastic inheritance rights of many corporations — Galivarian, especially — they *were* royal houses. An ancient story from Terra spoke of a future where royal houses ruled worlds; perhaps the author was a prophet touched by the Akashic.

"Nothing in this stack," Ajax said. "Next one."

Chibi obliged, barely shaken from his thoughts. He wondered what it would be like to be immortal. He pondered what the Demigods saw. He'd heard some of them were over a thousand years old. If that was true, then they'd watched the rise of the Empyrean Union. They had borne witness to the civil wars of the Outer Ring and Far Reach. Watched life and civilization scatter across the systems as governments rose and fell, worlds were built and destroyed, and entire races were wiped clean. How feeble life must seem to them . . . to live forever, detached from the world . . . it was precisely what Ajax wanted to escape.

"I've hit something," Ajax said. "I just got something like thirty-two hits for my query."

"Spill," Key ordered.

"I'd be faster if you let me focus," Ajax chided.

Chibi heard an alarm go off, the lights in the server room flashing red.

"Shit!" Ajax shouted. "I tripped something!"

"Get out of there!" Key commanded. "You've got no more than three minutes before Zaibatsu security will be on your ass!"

Chibi didn't waste a second, leaping to his feet and fleeing the server room. He slid as he tried to corner out the door towards the elevator.

"The receiver!"

He whirled back, trying to pull the device from the server.

"I can't get the receiver out!" he yelled. "What happens if I break it!?"

"Forget the receiver!" Key shouted. "Get out of there *now*!"

Chibi tugged again.

"It's locked in!" Ajax screamed. "They want to keep the connection locked! Just run!"

Chibi clenched his teeth and made another life-changing decision.

KEY STARTED to panic as everything went to shit in front of him. He was no hacker, but he knew that leaving the receiver was a dangerous move.

"What does it mean that you're locked in?" he asked.

"Kigen is fighting to trace me," Ajax replied. "They locked the receiver so that we couldn't disconnect and locked my connection to their network."

"What can you do about it?" Key asked.

"What can *we* do about it?" Six corrected.

"Not much," Ajax admitted. "I'm jumping from VPN to VPN, throwing proxies, just trying to cloak myself and escape, but they're chasing hard."

"How can we—"

Key was interrupted by a metal hand in his face telling him to stop.

"My brain is the computer, so shut up!" Ajax yelled. "If you distract me, I'm slow. If they catch me, I'm fried. If they fry me, I will actually die!"

Key sat in silence, bouncing his legs again. He wasn't sure if the tic predated his life as Key, but it was a tough one to stop. He dared not speak again — too much at risk. He'd been friends with Ajax basically since he was "reborn." He had helped the Oran find an old chat-box some fifty-year smoker had tossed out so he could have a voice instead of synthetic humming to imitate words. He owed Ajax for being the one to crack enough code on his spine for Six to integrate. He'd been the one to save Key's body.

"Fucking hell . . ." Ajax moaned. "They got a worm in me!"

"What!?" Key leapt to his feet.

"I should have known there'd be more than one trap!"

"They trapped the file with a worm?" Key asked. "What the hell did we find?"

"Shut up!" Ajax yelled.

Key fell silent again.

"Wait . . ." Ajax said. "I just . . . I disconnected?"

CHIBI WAS a bit out of breath. He'd spent a solid minute jamming his umbrella into the server tower. He heard the commotion over the comms, whaling on it with all his might, but his might was running out.

"I just . . . I disconnected?"

Chibi silently cheered, taking a deep, relieved breath. The server sparked and buzzed, the holes he'd punched in it with the metal tip aglow with electricity.

"I broke the server," Chibi panted.

"Then run, fucker, run!" Ajax yelled.

Chibi gripped his umbrella tight and took off down the hall. He got in the elevator, slowly descending.

Gwwrrrr . . .tht

The elevator jolted to a stop. Chibi panicked. He didn't have a gun and, more importantly, he didn't have backup.

Ka-thunk

Shit.

Something had landed on the roof of the elevator. From the sound of it and the slight shake, Chibi would have wagered it was a person.

Ka-thunk

Make that two.

BOOM!

The top of the elevator exploded, filling Chibi's ears with a shrill ringing. Between the flash and the dust, he couldn't see anything. He held his hands in front of his face and squinted. He wasn't sure if he was dizzy from the concussion blast or if the elevator car was actually shaking, but he was unbalanced regardless.

"Get him!" a voice outside Chibi's view commanded. "Live capture!"

At least they wanted him alive. There wasn't much that Chibi could do about it. He decided to go down with dignity, getting on his knees with his hands behind his head.

Ka-thunk ka-thunk

The two men dropped into the elevator, shaking it as they landed. They threw a blindfold over Chibi's eyes, taking limited visibility to none.

"What's going on?" Ajax asked over the comm. "We heard a lot of noise."

The men must have heard that, ripping the comm from Chibi's ear.

At least I got to do something before I died.

A shot in his neck and Chibi started slipping away. He had few thoughts but no fear. He didn't know when he'd die — not then — but he knew it would be soon. They weren't capturing him alive out of mercy; there was a reason they wanted him. He had no idea why he'd gotten off the train, but he knew exactly why he ran back.

He didn't regret it at all.

CHAPTER 23
A HUNT IS MORE THRILLING

"Chibi!" Ajax yelled.

"Shio!" Six shouted.

They heard the blast. They knew something bad was happening, but they weren't sure what. They had been prepared for Med-Sec to show up — they were monitoring *their* comms — but a trap was something they weren't ready for. Key was scrambling to try and get on the Kigen frequency, but he wasn't getting anywhere.

"Why the hell was the file trapped!?" Key asked, typing furiously.

"I'll explain when we get Chibi out of this mess!" Ajax yelled back. "Chibi, are you there?"

The three were met with silence. Then, a rustling came over the comm.

"I don't know who you are, or where you are . . . yet."

A stranger had taken Chibi's comm. The voice was distorted from the damage the microphone took in the blast, but it was clearly male. It was safe to assume it was one of the guys responsible for the blast — some heavy-hitting Kigen crony.

"The fuck you want?" Key spat.

"Your whole operation," the man replied. "You're stepping

into things you don't belong in and someone's gotta put you in your place."

"And you're the one to do it?"

"Maybe," the man chuckled. "Why don't you come to the front door and we can find out?"

"Not feeling that," Key replied.

"That's fine," the man said. "A hunt is more thrilling anyway."

"You couldn't stop us getting in the front door," Key taunted. "What makes you think you'll get us next time?"

"Med-Sec was the one after you before," the man said. "They failed to take you down, but we won't. You wouldn't believe the monster you just woke up."

"*Sore o nugu*."

Chibi's blindfold was taken off — more like torn off — revealing a man in a gilded suit. It looked to be a black velvet jacket with gold paisley and buttons. His shirt was also black, and he wore a gold tie, hanging loosely about his neck. His pants were white and shoes gold. Most striking were his all-gold prosthetics. His hands, chest, and even eyes were all glittering gold. Though he had the same fashion sense as Enoch, Chibi got the immediate sense that this guy played in a different league than the Sundowners Chibi had been hanging out with.

"*Kōgeki*."

A punch landed squarely on Chibi's cheek.

"*Mata*."

Another punch split his cheek open. Chibi tried to take in his surroundings as much as possible. He had tried to count intersections and turns to make a mental map and figure out where he was going during the ride over, but it was no use. He was convinced that only happened in movies.

"Who, pray tell, are you?" the gilded man asked, kneeling in front of Chibi.

The man had prominent cheekbones and a thin, regal nose. He'd have been handsome if he weren't so intimidating. Chibi stared in stunned silence.

"Mata."

Another strike, this time to the back of the head. Chibi was a little dazed after that one.

"Why were you in our server room?"

The man spoke to him in perfect Empyrean but gave commands in Japanese. This was hardly uncommon among the upper echelon, as Japan was crucial in the settling of Galivaria and even the Gali slang of a lot of the Sundowners was a bastardized form of the language, but it was definitely an indicator of the upper class. This guy was in a different league.

"Who are you?" Chibi asked. "Can we start there?"

The man stood, looking a little incensed but not furious.

"I am Kigen Katsuwara."

Chibi's heart sank. He had really dropped a hornets' nest on his head. In front of him was the eldest son of Matsuhide Kigen — the CEO and de facto king of Kigen Technologies. If Kigen was a country, Katsuwara was its prince.

"Now, who are you?" Katsuwara asked again. "And why have you done this?"

"I'm Chibi, and —"

A punch interrupted him.

"No," Katsuwara commanded. "Give me your *real,* given name."

Chibi stayed silent. He wanted to be defiant and hard, but he could feel the façade slipping.

"Mata."

Chibi received another punch as one of the thugs handed Katsuwara Chibi's ID badge.

"Ah," Katsuwara said. "Shimada Sukoshio."

There was a heavy moment as Chibi hung his head.

"So, not just a spy and a thief but a traitor, too," Katsuwara said. "Tell me, Suko . . . what made you turn your back on the Kigen family that had treated you so well?"

"You turned your backs first," Chibi retorted.

Katsuwara looked confused.

"Kare wa nani no desuka?"

"Wakaranai," the thug replied, clearly a little more than a thug.

"You guys tried to kill me first," Chibi said. "Your jackboots shot me because I followed some guy on the train."

"I do not have the first semblance of an idea what you are talking about," Katsuwara said.

"You blew up a train!" Chibi yelled.

"Nani desuka?"

"Med-Sec *ga bakuhatsu o hikiokoshita to kiita."*

Chibi sure didn't speak Japanese, but he heard "Med-Sec."

"Yeah, Med-Sec!" he shouted. "You and your Med-Sec cronies blew up a fucking train to try and kill one guy. News flash, he lived!" His voice rose. "I lived, too, but your buddies shot me in the head! Lucky me, Key was there to save the day."

"Who is this 'Key' individual?" Katsuwara asked.

"I don't really know," Chibi answered honestly. "He's a Detective you guys tried to fucking kill for some reason."

"I know nothing of a 'Key'," Katsuwara informed him, "but if he's one of your coconspirators, we will be finding him quite soon."

"Good luck," Chibi said. "Dude can't even find himself."

"Mata."

That punch split Chibi's eyebrow, blood trickling down his face.

"I don't much care for insolence, you see," Katsuwara said. "Still, our trap worked well enough, I'm sure, and you gave us something far larger to pursue."

Katsuwara removed his blazer, handing it off to one of his men, and rolled up the sleeves of his shirt.

"Killing you would be in poor taste, given the precious gift of information you have provided, so you get to live, but I assure you that sending you back to your friends will not make you any safer."

"Let me go and you'll never see me again," Chibi vowed.

He meant the words to sound brave but had the sneaking suspicion that they may have been a bad idea.

He was going to let you go! Why the hell would you say something?

"Believe that if you wish," Katsuwara said. "But before you go, there is still a price to be paid."

He drew a glinting black blade. His hand flexed and the edge of the blade erupted in red energy, a soft pulse and crackle reaching Chibi's ears.

"*Tsukamu*," he said.

Two thugs grabbed Chibi's arms.

"You were a member of my family, Shimada," Katsuwara said. "My house fed and clothed you, we gave you purpose and value."

Chibi lifted his chin defiantly. "You made me a husk of a man and only paid me enough to survive."

"You worked in Zaibatsu, our crown jewel," Katsuwara said. "You were in the very heart of my family — a place many would kill to be."

Chibi had honestly never thought about it. He worked in Zaibatsu; he worked for *the* Kigen office. That wasn't the tiny deal he often made it. Granted, he doubted any of the people who actually worked in Zaibatsu thought about it that much.

"For your deeply unfortunate betrayal of our family," Katsuwara said, "a price must be paid."

The thugs pulled Chibi's arms out from his sides as Katsuwara raised his sword. Chibi tried to resist, but the thugs were far stronger. Fighting a wave of panic, he forced himself to remain still. At least if the cuts were clean, he'd be in less pain afterwards. Katsuwara readied to bring down the sword.

"We shall see you again."

CHAPTER 24
WHO'S TO SAY

Key, Six, and Ajax went back to the apartment to rest and regroup. It didn't amount to much; none of them could sleep. Granted, Ajax never slept anyway. They knew they had to think. They had to take a step and make sure they were moving forward in the best way.

Chibi had sacrificed himself to make sure that Ajax was safe and the three of them weren't tracked. They didn't know what happened to him, but they knew they needed to do something about it. If it was vengeance, so be it.

"He might be dead," Key said.

"He might be," Ajax agreed, "but your pessimism isn't particularly helpful."

"It's my fault, though!" Key shouted, voice echoing in the quiet of the night. "I asked him to do this! I came up with the half-baked plan and ran us in there!"

"Key . . ." Six started, trying to calm him with a touch on his arm. "We all went along with it. We all participated."

"Chibi is a grown-ass man," Ajax said. "If he didn't want to do it, he didn't have to. He did."

Silence fell. Key wanted to rant and rave, but he knew that was just nervous energy and guilt. A lot of things were swirling in his head, but none of them were helpful. That changed little, but it kept him quiet.

"We told him to run," Ajax added. "He chose to turn around and smash the server."

"He was doing what he thought was right," Six said. "What he believed was best."

"And he did it for you," Ajax chimed in, "so don't invalidate that with some bullshit guilt."

"You're right," Key admitted. "Guilt isn't going to help him get out of this."

"Sir?"

The three of them nearly had a collective heart attack when Jeeves spoke.

"Yes, Jeeves?" Key replied.

"As requested, I have been monitoring Mr. Chibi's apartment."

"And?" Ajax asked.

"A body was just delivered outside the building. An analysis of the image would indicate that it is, in fact, Mr. Chibi."

Key leaped to his feet and grabbed his raincoat.

CHIBI SAT in the rain outside of his old apartment. He'd been dumped on the sidewalk like so much garbage; that's probably what Kigen thought of him. He cried, tears mixing with raindrops. His heart raced as he tried desperately to slow it. He looked at his arms, dismembered and tied around his neck like a macabre accessory. His mind was hazy. He tried to focus on a thought, bring in a singular focus to keep him awake.

They'll come . . . he assured himself. *They'll come for sure.*

Ten minutes passed. Then another ten. Chibi grew colder. He hoped it wasn't blood loss. The Kigen guys had bandaged his stumps, but who's to say if it was effective.

"That's it . . ." he whispered hoarsely through chapped lips. "Shio Shimada is truly dead."

KEY DIDN'T EVEN BOTHER to get in a car, choosing instead to run through the deluge. His raincoat meant nothing after only a few minutes, his every step splashing up so much water that his pants were already soaked and his shirt wasn't far behind. After a kilometer or so, a car came up next to him.

"Get in."

Key hopped in the back seat.

"You made it three blocks and you're completely soaked," Ajax said. "Would it have killed you to think for half a second before taking off?"

"I just . . ."

"Stop feeling guilty!" Ajax screamed. "Chibi made his own choices and he chose to help *your* sorry ass!"

"I appreciate that," Key said, a little humbled by Ajax's outburst. "I couldn't do it alone."

"That's the idea," Six said. "So just accept the help, already."

CHIBI SAT ON THE CURB, shivering. He was scared to move for fear of opening his wounds, but he decided to scoot towards the awning of his building. Safe from the rain, he desperately clung to what thoughts he could muster. He didn't want to die. He wasn't ready to die. He had to *choose* to live. A little delirious, perhaps, he was finally ready to make another choice: he was going to become a Black Angel.

Six wove in and out of traffic so fast that hydroplaning was inevitable. Key was surprised at the number of cars in the streets. The middle of the night, during a proper downpour, after the end of the workweek was hardly peak rush hour. The traffic wasn't heavy — only enough to give Key a heart attack every time his wife barreled towards an oncoming vehicle.

Though without her driving like a maniac, they might not have made it to Chibi in time.

Whether the rain or the bleeding, Chibi could feel himself fading. His eyelids grew heavy as his head spun. He doubted it was hypothermia.

Well . . . it certainly wasn't ordinary.

He faintly heard a car pull up and the splash of footsteps.

"ChIbi!"

His hearing was distorted, so he couldn't make out who was talking. His sight didn't help.

"wE'VE Got YOu!"

He slipped in and out, head pulsing and fingers numb.

But I don't have fingers . . .

CHAPTER 25
YAKUZA WANNABE

Key had never really watched Six work. He still had PTSD from when he underwent surgery himself — probably mixed with the suppressed memories of the experiments — so he rarely was even in the building when she had a patient on the table. But for Chibi, he made an exception. A *big* exception.

"Patient had severe third-degree burn damage to the fore-arm," Six said, dictating her notes. "Patient required two trans-humeral amputations."

She handed Key the bonesaw, still dripping with blood.

"Hemostat."

Key did as he was told, grabbing the ratcheted pliers from the tray. Six took them, clamping a vessel in Chibi's arm. The *click* of the forceps locking into place caused a pang of anxiety.

"Hemostat."

Again, he handed it over.

"Ajax," Six started, "have you prepared the arms for cali-bration?"

"Just about."

"Tenaculum."

Key grew nauseous as he grabbed the clawed device. He knew what she was about to do.

"I'm extracting the nerves," she said. "I need those arms to be ready."

Ajax gave a silent salute. Key turned away as Six reached into Chibi's stumps and pulled out the tips of nerves. Waves of nausea came over him. He tried to breathe deeply. His nose filled with the smell of alcohol, formaldehyde, and blood, weakening his knees.

"Patient is stable."

He knew it was a hallucination — a memory forcing its way into reality — but he couldn't stop it. The smell made him gag as he lost touch with the present.

"I need a spinal retractor."

Phantom pains danced across his back, making his fingers and toes tingle. He vomited, the retching breaking him from his daze.

"Go to the office!" Six shouted, abnormally harsh. "Go now!"

Key stumbled out of the room. He knew she was right. An operating room was no place for bile.

Why was I even in there? he wondered. *I knew something like this would happen.*

He went to the office as instructed, throwing himself onto the old blue couch. He curled up as the memories kept spinning in his mind.

"Everything is going to be fine," the voice said.

He recognized the voice, a nagging familiarity that was impossible to put a finger on. Was it a colleague? He still didn't know who Heihachi was — who *he* was — but, after everything settled, they'd look at the files. They'd find something.

We have to find something.

That was the only way Key could see a silver lining to the situation. If Chibi lost his arms *and* they came up with nothing, there was no way he'd be able to forgive himself. If nothing else, they knew he was a Kigen man before they tossed him out. At least he'd be able to empathize with Chibi.

"Our boy pulled through," Ajax said, ducking to enter the office. "Only minor complications to come."

"Such as?"

Key hated being present for surgery, but discussing it never bothered him. Good thing, given the family business.

"Not 100 percent sure," Ajax answered. "But you saw the wounds. His arms were *burned* off."

"Awfully cruel of them to leave him holding the burned-off arms," Key muttered. "But at least that stanched the bleeding and cauterized the stumps."

"Fuckin' Yakuza wannabe . . ."

"I don't think they're really 'wannabes', Jax," Key said, trying to break out of his daze. "Seems to me anybody that does shit like this just *is*."

"I guess."

There was a beat or two of silence before Key spoke up.

"How's your head?"

"You mean the worm?" Ajax asked.

Key nodded.

"I've got it sandboxed," Ajax said. "It's still active, but it's not going anywhere else."

"What is it, then?"

"It's got some lines of nav code and a satellite connection, so I'm guessing it's a tracker."

"So Kigen knows where we are?"

Ajax laughed. "Like they couldn't have found us anyway."

Six came into the office. "Got him fixed up and knocked out," she said. "He should stay down until tomorrow morning at least."

"We staying here?" Ajax asked.

"We have to," Six answered. "Doc is off-world and Swift and Birdie are over in Omakasu."

"So, there's no one to watch the clinic," Ajax said. "And, more importantly, Chibi."

Key nodded.

"Guess we'd better get comfortable."

MORNING CAME IN A BLINK. It seemed the last few days had taken their toll; Key was more tired than he thought. He honestly didn't even remember falling asleep. He had sat in the office, talking and laughing with Six and Ajax until he passed out on the couch. He looked up to see Ajax sitting in the chair opposite the desk.

"You're awake," Ajax said.

"So are you."

"I'm always awake."

"True enough," Key chuckled.

He tried his best to slide out from under Six's flopped-over head. She'd fallen asleep on him and he preferred not to wake her.

"I assume you paid Chibi a visit?"

"A few," Ajax said. "He's stable."

"She's a good surgeon," Key said, patting his arm for illustration. "I knew he would be."

"I ran diagnostics to make sure his arms were receiving the signals they needed."

"I assume they were fine."

"Not quite," Ajax confessed, "Six did an amazing job salvaging what she could, but there was a lot of damage."

"How much?"

"He'll probably be able to figure it out," Ajax said. "But he's not going to be the platinum standard for post-op recovery. Gold at best."

"Gimme a little more, here," Key said. "I don't want to have to fill in the blanks."

"Even with physical therapy, he's not likely to get over 70 percent functionality," Ajax said. "He'll be able to get a lot of stuff to be natural and instinctual, but he'll have to put actual thought into some things."

Key's countenance fell.

"I know that look, damn it," Ajax fumed. "He *chose* to make this sacrifice for us. Don't you dare rob him of that with your guilt."

"I know," Key acknowledged, "but I can still feel pain for a friend."

CHAPTER 26
THE NAME I CHOSE

Chibi had only the vaguest awareness of where he was and what was happening. He remembered being in front of his apartment, someone picking him up, and then being in a hospital. That was roughly it. He recalled searing pain in his fingertips but not much else. Then he blinked awake.

"Hello?" he whispered hoarsely.

His vision was incredibly blurry, but each blink brought the world more into focus. He saw a sterile, white tiled room, dimly lit by florescent lights along the wall. He felt the faintest tingling in his hands.

But I don't have hands . . .

He went to look at his stumps and saw metal arms instead. Maybe it was the dissonance, or maybe the drugs had yet to wear off. Either way, Chibi started to have a panic attack.

BEEEEEEEEP

An alarm sounded through the room. Not blaring but loud enough to grab attention. Chibi glanced over at a panel on the wall, realizing the alarm was linked to his vitals. That didn't particularly help — he was still hyperventilating — but it at least put things in context.

Where am I? What happened? Who has me? What are these machines!?

His mind raced. It seemed possible that Kigen had picked him up again — but unlikely. Katsuwara said he had bigger fish to fry.

Breathe . . . he thought, struggling to calm down. *Just breathe through it.*

He knew panicking wasn't going to help. The alarm only made it worse.

Breathe!

Six, Key, and Ajax burst through the doors on the far wall. Whether they were rescuing him or already had, seeing them was a relief in its own right.

"What's wrong!?" Six shouted. "Are you okay?!"

She scrambled, moving his gown around — he only just realized he was wearing one — checking the sensor pads. She shined a light in his eye.

"I'm fine," Chibi said, trying to gently push her away.

"Trying" was the all-important word, as he found himself unable to move his arm to do so. He focused on it and his arm sluggishly responded.

"What's wrong with me?" he asked.

"Severe nerve damage," Ajax said, mild pain in his voice.

"What happened to 'indistinguishable from the real thing' . . .?" Chibi asked, trying to joke.

No one laughed.

"I thought we could regrow nerves and shit," Chibi said. "Stem cells and all that."

"That's . . . expensive technology," Six confessed. "Not to mention that I'm a surgeon, not a bio-fabricator."

"So . . . what?" Chibi asked in disbelief. "This is it? I'm stuck with this?"

"In time," Key explained, "you'll get better control. It takes a little while."

Chibi nodded solemnly.

"I did what I did," he said. "I could have saved myself, but this is a small price to pay for Ajax's life."

Ajax held out his hand. With some concerted effort, Chibi took it.

"You wanted to be part of the team," Ajax said. "I'd say you're more than there."

A warmth radiated through Chibi's chest. It felt good to be a part of the team — to belong.

"I want to be a Black Angel," he said.

He made the choice while having an out-of-body moment on his stoop, nearly succumbing to his wounds, but he stood by it. He'd floated through life long enough. It was time to take charge and become something more.

"I mean —"

Chibi was interrupted by a hand on his chest.

"Start by being you," Six retorted.

Chibi wasn't quite prepared for that response.

I'm always me . . . he thought.

Six pulled over a stool, sitting at his bedside.

"Let me tell you about yourself," she said. "Stop me if I'm wrong."

Chibi braced himself for some harsh truths, but he nodded.

"You were born to moderately affluent parents," she began. "They raised with you with love but not a lot of affirmation; you were always expected to reach higher, do better, and become more."

Chibi swallowed hard.

"In sports, you were great. In academics, you were great. You were a people person — magnetic and charming."

These were compliments — or at least they should have been — but they stung Chibi for some reason. Why did they hurt?

"In college, you had friends. You had girlfriends. You had promise."

So far, so spot on. Six was hitting the nail on the head.

"Then . . . you graduated."

Chibi's heart sank.

"You got your first job — a big and bright one to match your big, bright potential," Six said. "I'd bet your dad even put in a good word for you."

Chibi hadn't thought about his parents for a while. He missed them.

"That's when everything fell apart for you."

I kept it together . . . Chibi thought stubbornly. *I didn't fall apart.*

"You had spent twenty-two years living up to everyone else's expectations, fitting their mold and measuring up, and you didn't know what to do," Six said, genuine concern in her voice. "You had looked forward for so long that, when you actually got to where you were going, you were lost."

Lost . . .

That was probably one of the most accurate words to describe Chibi. He had been completely directionless. Purposeless.

"With no direction, you underperformed. You lost your job."

Got me there.

"After that, you felt defeated," Six said. "You'd never really felt a wall in front of you before. So, rather than self-reflect, you threw yourself at that wall. Eventually, you gave up and settled into monotonous nothingness."

Damn.

"Through all of it, it was never something you did for yourself. You were trying to live up to the expectations of teachers, parents, and bosses, but never you."

Chibi felt accused. He probably should have been.

"Even the short time I've known you, you've been clinging to names and titles."

"Yeah . . ." Chibi said, voice weak.

"When you got burned, you decided you were dead," Six

said. "I know Key and Enoch weren't exactly helpful with your process there, but it was telling to me; your job was your life."

"Yeah . . ." Chibi said again, nodding.

"Shimada or Chibi, you're still *you*," Six said, "but I don't think you really know what that means."

"I know who I am," Chibi said defensively.

Six looked at him with anticipation.

"I . . . I'm . . ."

"It's no good to find your identity in other people," Six said. "You have to find it within yourself."

"I'm Chibi," he answered. "That's the name I chose for myself."

"That's a start," Six said encouragingly. "What does it mean to be 'Chibi'?"

"I'm loyal," Chibi said. "And when I tell people I'm going to do something, I do it."

"Sounds good," Six said, smiling.

Key smiled, turning. Chibi stared at the angel on his back.

"I'm out," Key said.

"Who are *you*?" Chibi asked.

Key froze. He turned, slowly. There was a masked look of terror on his face, deep pain in his eyes.

"I don't know."

Chibi could see a look of near-panic rise on Key's face. He had meant the question innocently enough — it *was* the topic at hand — but the emotions were undeniable.

"I do," Six said.

Key looked a little shaken. He tugged at his sleeve.

"I could say the same thing to you that I said to Chibi," she continued. "I've been trying to for years and I'm getting really tired of the same fucking conversation."

There was a palpable pressure in the room. Chibi was not about to get in the middle of this.

"I don't give a shit or even half a fuck who you *used* to be," she said. "You are who you choose to be, and that's who you are now."

"So, who is that?" Key asked. "Who am I?"

"That's what you need to figure out," Six said. "I know, but telling you does no good."

Key looked shocked at the reply.

"You proved to me just now that all the things I've been saying for three years *can* take root in your thick skull, but I'm not going to waste my breath," Six said. "You have to figure it out for yourself."

Chibi watched Key's heart sink. He looked to the floor, unable to hold Six's pained and piercing gaze.

"Okay."

Key rubbed his nose with his sleeve and left, punctuated by the door's squeaky hinge. Six turned back to Chibi, placing a hand on his arm.

"You rest up," she said, masking her pain with a smile and a chipper tone. "I'll be back in a bit."

As she left, she grabbed a coffee cup from the counter on the left side of the room, filling it with water and placing it on the tray table beside Chibi.

"If you feel up to it," she said, "try to pick up that mug and drink."

Chibi nodded. Six nodded back.

"Good," she said, turning and leaving the room.

Ajax stood in silence, arms hanging at his sides. Without expressions to read, his quiet was disconcerting. There was nothing to clue Chibi in to what was going on in his head. He decided he should break the stillness.

"I figured out what replacement part I'm getting you first," he said.

"Oh?" Ajax replied, voice more upbeat than Chibi expected. "What part is that?" — he held up his claw machine hands — "Actual fingers?"

"Nah," Chibi laughed. "We gotta get you a face."

Ajax laughed, patting Chibi's leg.

"Take a nap or something." he said. "I hear those help with the healing."

He, too, left, Chibi alone with his thoughts. He looked at his hands, the blue-tinted metal and rubberized padding sitting as a mockery in his lap.

What was the point . . .? he asked himself.

What had been a comfort not even a day ago — the belief that he had done something good, that he had mattered somehow — was fading. Now he wondered if he was more a liability than anything else. Six may have meant what she said to be encouraging, but the words bit deep. He didn't know what he was doing. He had no idea how to be a gangster, hacker, or Detective. He was just . . . Sukoshio Shimada, well-educated nobody.

Are they going to let me in? Or have I served my purpose to them?

He chided himself for the dark thought. He knew them better than that. They weren't the type to use-abuse-and-lose a person. He had been alone for so long that it was hard to have faith in others. He'd relied on himself — but not anymore. Enoch had given him the clothes on his back. Key and Six had fixed him up when leaving him to die would have been a lot easier. Safer, too.

He laboriously wiggled his fingers, the final nail in Sukoshio Shimada's coffin. He pondered what losing his old life meant. He had resisted his change in large part. Everything was happening so fast, he could be forgiven for it not settling in, but that time was gone. He'd never truly let go of Shio. He gave himself a new name and donned the trappings, but he was trying to repay a debt. It was like he told Ajax:

"I can't be too disparaging . . . I owe them both my life."

He kind of owed Enoch, too. But that was the thing — he owed them. He was still harboring a grudge against Key for what happened. He was a reluctant participant, a tag-along. He went into the Underground because he was told to. He went to Zaibatsu because he was told to. He may have wanted to be an equal part of the team, but he was still a cynic. He didn't help because he was passionate; he did it because he couldn't go home — something he still blamed Key for. Now . . . there was no one to blame. He *chose* to run back. That got him caught. That lost him his arms.

His old life stared him in the face and called him a traitor.

CHAPTER 27
PROGRESS

Key walked and walked. He hadn't grabbed his raincoat on the way out, but the previous night's downpour left the clouds anemic by Galivarian standards. The air barely even had a mist, leaving everything cold and wet, but it spared him from getting soaked. Not that he would have noticed; he was too lost in thought to care.

Who am I? he asked. *For so long, it's been 'who was I', but Six is right . . . I'm different, now.*

Deep down, he'd always known that, but it was a truth that demanded more than just knowledge; he needed to understand. Now that he did, he was frustrated it had taken him so long. At the same time, it made him wonder why he suddenly did.

Am I just scared of the past?

He'd never thought of himself as a coward. He wasn't the type to run away. Yet when he faced down his past, he was filled with terror. If the Bartender was any source of wisdom, it was probably his subconscious mind trying to tell him not to seek out the pain. After all, he'd locked the memories away for a reason, right?

What made me who I was? What made me who I am?

Key may have been pondering some of the fundamental

principles of existence itself, but he wasn't getting anywhere. He was far from stupid, but he never really sat down and tried to logic out mortal nature and the concepts of what makes a person. Still, as a Detective — a fundamentally curious mind — the train of thought was something he embraced.

I was a blank slate when Six found me. So who I am was very much shaped by who she is, right? That's how that nature and nurture stuff works.

He puzzled it over as he walked, no destination in mind but plenty of thoughts to distract him.

Six said I have to figure out who I am . . . She already gets it . . . Why is it so hard for me?

He found himself in Nakama, the lower merchant district. Everything was pretty quiet, only a few vendors actively selling their wares. A young woman stood under an awning, her hair bright pink and lips black, selling tee shirts with graphic designs, and a man sitting inside his shop shouting about how he had fresh soup. Key's stomach growled.

"All your essentials!" the man shouted. "Bone broth, eggs, and rice!"

Key ducked into the little shop and slid into a booth at the back. He always felt kind of silly about it, but he hated to have his back to people. He made eye contact with the cook and raised his hand, nodding slightly. In a minute or so, the store crier brought over a bowl of a steaming soup. He hadn't been lying; the soup smelled delicious.

"Enjoy," the man said, resuming his "advertisement" by the door.

Key dug in, savory delights filling his hungry stomach. He couldn't remember the last meal he'd actually eaten, but it had probably been well over twelve hours. Maybe that was why the soup tasted so good. In the end, it didn't matter much. Key wolfed down his bowl before holding up his hand for another. With a big smile, the crier brought him a second bowl.

The name I choose for myself . . . Key thought, recalling Chibi's words that morning. *I didn't get to choose to become Key.*

He'd never felt resentment over the loss of his memory, just a nagging urge to rediscover himself. Somehow, the realization of how powerless and infinitesimal he was even in his own rebirth hit him like a ton of bricks.

I chose my name. I didn't choose to forget, but I chose who I am now.

Progress.

Beep beep boopadoo boop. Beep beep boopadoo boop.

Key's phone was ringing. Though it was incredibly convenient sometimes, he occasionally wished he hadn't had the receiver implanted in his head.

"What's up?" he asked.

"I've been going over the files I was able to extract from . . . you know," said Ajax on the other end. "I've um . . . I've found some heavy shit."

"Spill."

"I'd rather not talk about it over an open channel," Ajax replied. "Come on back to the apartment and I'll fill you in."

"Six and Chibi there?"

"Yeah," Ajax said. "She gave him the official clearance to leave the clinic, so we three came back."

"I'll head back then."

Key drank the last of his broth and rose to his feet, tapping the back of his hand on the glowing pad on the end of the table. The pad lit up green, as did a circle on his hand, and Key departed, giving a courteous nod and wave to the cook and crier.

"Come back any time!"

CHIBI SPENT the rest of the day in his first physical therapy treatments. If just shaking Ajax's hand was a challenge, he had a lot of work to do figuring out how to use his bionics. So, with new set of clothes and Six as a therapist, he got to work.

He found his arms were not as advertised. They were simultaneously much more reactive than a flesh-and-blood version, while also being sluggish and hard to move. Not to mention *much* heavier. Each arm must have weighed seven kilos, though they made up for it with strength. With a little more practice, they might have been helpful, but five hours and seven shattered coffee mugs later, he was about fed up. That frustration brought up other things with it, boiling from within him. He felt like a liability — dead weight. The joy of surviving wore off, supplanted by a hollow sense of going past square one and into the negatives.

As the day waned, so did his patience. Six decided it was time to end for the night. He sat in a wood-paneled room with a single table and four chairs, angrily staring at a cup he wanted desperately to drink from but couldn't lift. He almost didn't notice Six sit beside him.

"At least you made progress," she said, trying to be encouraging.

He focused on tapping his fingers on the table, making increasingly deeper dents.

"So . . ." she began. "Let's talk some more about you wanting to be a Black Angel."

"I can't yet." The words barely made it past his clenched teeth.

"Well, sure, but —"

"I'm useless!" he spat. "I got my arms chopped off for nothing!"

Six recoiled slightly. Chibi felt immediately guilty. He wasn't *entirely* sure where the rage was even coming from. A few hours ago, he felt fine — depressed if anything — but now he was just . . . angry.

"Ajax has a worm in his system, we're all on Kigen's hit list, and I can barely function on my own," he said, calming down but no less distressed.

Six sat in silence for a moment. Chibi worried he had upset her.

"What is your name?" he asked. "I know your surgeon parents didn't look at you and say 'yup, gonna name that baby Six, dear'."

"No," she said, staring through the table. "That was a name the boys gave me; we named each other."

"And they named you Six?"

"No," she said again. "Riser — my brother Rin — gave me some other name I can't remember now."

"Then how . . .?"

"My shirt," she answered. "I had a favorite shirt with a big number six on it, so Swiftie started calling me by that. For some reason I liked it better." She paused. "We were younger then, y'know?"

"So, what is your name, Six?" Chibi asked. "Have I earned the privilege of learning your *mei*, yet?"

Six got very quiet and even more distant.

"You're one of us now, Chibi," she answered. "You put your life on the line for us."

"We're blood?"

Six nodded. She reached out and took his hand. He couldn't feel it, but he felt the emotion behind it. He knew where he belonged.

"My name is Natsu."

CHAPTER 28
SUPER-SECRET, PROBABLY ILLEGAL

Key arrived back at his home, a palpable weight in the room as he walked in. Everyone turned to look at him, concern and pain in their eyes. Though Ajax had no face to show it, his voice conveyed it as he spoke.

"How, uh . . . how are you?"

"Fine . . .?" Key replied, put off and confused. "What's going on? What did you find?"

"Well, like I said, I was combing through the files . . ." Ajax trailed off. "You guys have a blackout protocol? One less intense than Absolute Dark, I mean."

Key rolled his eyes. "Goddammit dude, yeah. Will you fucking spill already?"

He tapped the panel by the door.

"Sir?" Jarvis asked.

"Blackout, Jarvis," Key replied. "Shut down all outside access, Turtle Shell Protocol."

"Understood."

Key took a seat, clasping his hands in anticipation as the constant droning in his head fell silent, the endless feed of information pouring through his uplink blocked by a bubble of intangible stone.

The apartment had gone dark.

"I already told you about the first one," Ajax began tentatively. "Some mention of his name mixed into a document about corporate succession, but the later ones . . . the ones that were trapped . . ."

"Just come out with it!" Key demanded.

He shot to his feet gesturing wildly as his frustration reached a fever pitch. He couldn't have pinpointed what he was angry about, but it was coming to a boil.

"Geez! You guys are all dark-faced and shit and beating around the bush, and it's annoying the fucking shit out of me!" Key spat. "I hunted for this for the entirety of my remembered life — I *asked* for this. So, give me the fucking info or get out!"

He dropped back to the couch. The room was silent. Chibi squirmed uncomfortably, as Six hung her head in disappointment. That stung. Key was breathing hard, too embarrassed by his outburst to apologize, instead just gesturing for Ajax to continue. After a quiet that deepened Key's remorse, he did.

"The files were *super* fragmented, but I was able to reconstruct some of it," Ajax said. "Most of it was nonsense — just random words with no context — but I did find the name Project Prometheus in there, like you hoped. Looks like Heihachi was one of the scientists that worked on the project. I also did find mention of him betraying the company but no specifics."

"So, not much we didn't already know," Key said, an edge of despair creeping in. "We learned I was a scientist for Kigen, maybe one of the ones that built my spine, but that's only so much of a lead."

"I also learned some stuff," Chibi chimed in. "I won't say it's a lot, but while Kigen had me, I did learn some more about all this."

"Spill."

"Kigen has no idea who you are," Chibi said.

"How is that —" Key's confusion interrupted the thought. "*Someone* tried to kill me."

"Well, sure, but Katsuwara doesn't know you. Your name meant nothing to him," Chibi said. "They might have files on Heihachi, but Key isn't on their radar. Kigen isn't the one sending the jackboots after you."

Key's mind started to withdraw. He was zoning out, trying to piece together the mystery — the mystery of himself. It wasn't just a question of his past anymore, it was a matter of survival. Failure meant death. He had to figure out who was after him so that he could get them first.

I was supposed to create something for Kigen. Something happened and they tortured me instead. So how did I end up with the spine . . .?

It wasn't much.

Perhaps more importantly, if I died, they would have done asset recovery, so why do I ***still*** *have it?*

"Did you find any mention of my spine?"

"Nothing really, no," Ajax admitted. "Why? Do you think it was part of Project Prometheus?"

"It's the best idea I have," Key said. "It's the only prosthetic in my body without any identifying characteristics, not to mention that every piece of software in it is encrypted."

"Makes enough sense," Chibi said. "I never heard anything about encryptions when I worked at Kigen, so it's not exactly standard practice for them."

"I'd definitely want to encrypt my super-secret, probably illegal project," Ajax said.

Damn, Key thought. *Still nothing to show for all that everyone's done . . .*

"I, uh . . ." Key started, swallowing hard as he tried to muster the courage, "I'm sorry for what happened to you, Chibi — your arms, I mean."

No one spoke, all eyes on Chibi.

"You told me to run and I didn't," Chibi said.

"But the information we got —" Key said, pausing as he tried to tried to find the right words "— it just doesn't seem worth it."

"It was worth it to me, okay?" Chibi said defiantly.

"Okay," Key relented. "And . . . I'm sorry for exploding just now. I just —"

"You've taken a couple bullets to the head," Ajax interrupted. "Doesn't make your hissy fit less of a dick move, but I won't hold it against you."

Key looked to Chibi.

"You guys kept me from dying twice," he said. "I'm in no position to hold a grudge."

Key looked to Six.

"I get it," she said. "But next time you want to blow up, remember that we're the ones on your side."

Key nodded sheepishly. "I won't forget. And I won't do it again."

KEY DREAMED.

"Death is nothing to a god!"

He couldn't place the voice, but, as always, it was hauntingly familiar. Unlike so many, he was a mere observer of this dream. It was not him on the table but someone else. He stared down from his omniscient perch as the scientists cut the body to pieces. They brought new parts, filament tendrils reaching out of the corpse to grab the limbs that were offered. This cobbled together form was not strictly human: it had breasts and a penis, five eyes and four arms — two made of scrapped prostheses and random flesh. Though four of its eyes were closed, the central fifth eye stared. Key could feel their piercing gaze on him.

There is no option for failure.

The thought came from his mind but without his permission.

Katsuwara wants results.

The eyes of the creature flew open, a hideous shriek casting Key back to the waking world.

He was still . . . so . . . tired.

MORNING CAME AND WENT, pushing up on 15:00 before Key finally rolled out of bed. He'd slept like shit. Everyone was gone when he got up, leaving him alone with his thoughts.

He wasn't about to take what was coming lying down. He knew they were coming. He didn't know who "they" were — probably some gun-toting chrome-domes on Katsuwara's payroll — but it didn't really matter who was coming after him. Jackboot, Streetrunner, or Merc, Key was going to have to deal with it.

No time to waste.

KEY WALKED ALL the way to Kanpa. Six, Chibi, and Ajax were already sitting at the bar. Enoch stood behind it, pouring drinks for the rest. Key took a seat next to Six, Enoch sliding a drink his way.

"There's a storm coming," Key said solemnly.

"*Raijin* and *Fujin* playin' their games, *ne*?" Enoch asked, pouring a drink for himself.

"Looks like it," Ajax said, staring into his glass.

"We have to be ready," Chibi said, trying to be brave. "If they're coming, we have to be ready for them so we can strike back."

Key shook his head. "This is my fight."

"Like hell it is!" Six spat, turning to cast her indignant gaze directly at him. "Let's take stock, shall we?"

She held up her hand, ready to count.

"Chibi got his arms cut off." — A finger up — "Ajax got a worm in his system." — Another finger — "There's a manhunt for you." — A third — "It seems to me that the lot of us have some skin in this game."

Enoch, Chibi, and Ajax nodded in agreement.

"No way I'm losin' any *okini* to some *kaiju* fucks," Enoch said, lighting a cigarette. "They ain' after me yet, but they're gonna be when I'm done with the *gasayaro*."

Key's countenance dropped a bit. He didn't want them getting caught up in all of this. It was his tireless search for his past that launched this shit, and now they were all swept up in it. He thought about everything that had happened, the last couple weeks swirling in his mind. He thought about the train — the single event that ruined Chibi's life. He thought about the multiple attempts on his life, only foiled by the fact that he couldn't die. Now danger was closing in.

"Enoch?"

"*Hai*?"

Key took a long sip from his drink, taking Ajax's untouched glass and gulping that down, too.

"Do you trust Nat?"

Skepticism crossed Enoch's face as he cautiously poured Key another drink.

"She's been with me a *hottomin*, yeah."

"Did you tell her to send me to the Wires?"

"*Bangō*," Enoch said. "I never gave the green."

Key took another swig from his glass. He looked Enoch in the eyes, holding his stare for an uncomfortable length. Both men tried to read the other's mind. They'd been friends for a long time; it wasn't so hard to figure out what the other was thinking.

"You thinkin' she sent you to slaughter," Enoch said.

It should have been a question but it wasn't. They *had* been friends for a long time.

"I think I went to see people I haven't talked to in months, they had no idea why I was there, and then Med-Sec swooped in with guns and torch grenades."

"That's a steep finger to point," Enoch said. "Sounds a little flimsy."

"Have you seen her since Supe Ups?" Six asked, joining the conversation.

It broke some of the tension between Enoch and Key, the two finally ending their staring contest.

"*Bangō*," Enoch admitted. "I guessed she was on a binge again."

"Enoch."

Enoch locked eyes with Key again. Key's expression had changed. It wasn't a hard-nosed accusation anymore. In its place was a look of pain and fear.

"We can't risk a traitor."

Enoch's own steely gaze cracked a little.

"I'll look into it."

CHAPTER 29
A BULLET OR TWENTY

Enoch followed through on his word, and within a couple days he had Nat in his office. As always, Chibi was expected to be there.

"Where ya been, squib?" Enoch asked, taking a drag off his cigarette.

The meeting started casual enough. Despite the fact they had to track her down, Enoch clearly wasn't ready to start throwing around accusations.

"Is that really your business?" Nat asked. "We always said private was private."

"You've been straight *nai* for days," Enoch replied. "You've been missing work."

"I've had stuff," Nat said dismissively.

Chibi stood behind Enoch, arms behind his back, trying his best to look threatening. In truth, it was just because his arms were still so sluggish. Enoch leaned back, folding his hands and crossing his legs. Nat had a very different demeanor from the night Chibi met her. Then, she was confident and poised. She carried herself with sex appeal and power. Now, she sat in a chair opposite Enoch's desk, knees together and gaze cast to the floor. Though she was obviously trying to carry some of her previous bravado, shooting down the questions thrown her way, it was clear that she was scared.

"You had 'stuff', *ne*?" Enoch asked. "You swore me an oath — made a *yakusoku*."

Nat had no reply.

"Where the hell were you?"

"Y'know . . ." Nat muttered, trying to deflect again. "Sex, drugs, and synth, right?"

Standing behind Enoch, Chibi couldn't see his face, but he could feel the energy rising off of him. He could see the tension in his shoulders and hear the frustration in his voice.

"When I found you, you were a *shōfu* on a string of highs," Enoch said, tone low and voice tight. "I took you in, propped you up, made you my *hosa*, and put you to work."

"What's your point?" Nat asked, finally making eye contact.

"You're my *meinu!*" Enoch shouted, shooting from his chair and throwing his cigarette butt at her. "You're no *okini* or *kazo* to me! You ain' allowed to disappear!"

Nat looked almost betrayed.

"I've managed Kanpai for you for two years," she said, words weak as her eyes misted. "You're telling me I mean nothing to you?"

Enoch straightened up, calming slightly, but staying just as imposing.

"If I put you on a scale against Key?" he asked rhetorically. "The scale would fall over."

Tears brimmed from Nat's eyes.

"Where. The fuck. Were you."

Nat broke eye contact again. She wrung her hands, gripping her fingers so tightly they turned white.

"I was laying low," she confessed. "Just hiding at my place."

"*Detarame,*" Enoch muttered. "My guy spotted you gettin' dinner at Jiganshi."

Nat fell silent, caught in her lie.

"Did you sell Key to Med-Sec?" Enoch asked.

Nat didn't say anything.

"Nothing?"

Enoch dashed around the edge of his desk, pressing a gun to Nat's forehead.

"Did you sell my *kyodai* to the *kaiju!?*"

Nat burst into tears, hands up in surrender. Enoch pressed the gun harder, finger itching on the trigger. Chibi could feel his rage. He remained stoic in his place, trusting his boss — his *oyabun* — to do what needed to be done and nothing more.

"I didn't know!" Nat shrieked. "The Wires told me they had intel on some guy named Heihachi Hanamura and they wanted to talk to Key about it!"

Enoch stepped back, dropping the gun from her forehead. A red ring marked the skin.

"*Hontō* . . . they said that?" Enoch asked. "They told you *Heihachi Hanamura*?"

"Yes!" Nat screamed, still terrified.

"What did they drop on you?" Enoch asked.

"Beta told me they hacked Med-Sec after their run on Nu-U and they found something," she said. "They said that if Key didn't come talk to them about it, they'd leak the intel and we'd be swarmed with jackboots all kicking our teeth in."

"So you sent him to die."

"I didn't know Med-Sec was going to be there!" Nat protested. "I thought they wanted Key to investigate or something!"

Enoch leaned back, sitting on the edge of the desk.

"You were completely *muku, ne?*" Enoch asked. "No blood on your hands?"

"I promise," Nat assured him. "I didn't know Med-Sec was going to be there."

Enoch nodded. He stepped back behind his desk and took his seat.

"What'd ya get at Jiganshi?"

"What?" Nat asked, confused.

"The food," Enoch clarified. "Pretty nice, yeah?"

Nat nodded.

"Expensive, too."

Nat nodded.

"So, what'd you order?"

"Um . . . I got a black-fin sushi . . .?" Nat answered, a bit unsure. "Some sake, too."

"Ah! I love a good sake." Enoch smiled. "What kind?"

Chibi was just as confused as Nat. He was trying to puzzle out the sudden shift in not only topic but demeanor. All air of malice and rage had evaporated from Enoch, leaving only a conversational tone.

"It was a silver vine with plum," she answered.

"Ooo, *sugoi*," Enoch said. "Top shelf."

Nat nodded.

"How did you afford that?"

The color drained from Nat's face. Enoch's reasoning clicked in Chibi's mind.

"I . . . that is, I —"

"You had *okane* to spare, *ne?*" Enoch said. "I know I don' pay you that much."

"Enoch, I —"

"*Kite* . . . 'I-I-I'!" Enoch mocked. "You fuckin sold out my *kazo* — my *kyodai* — to Med-Sec for some gil."

Fear gripped Nat's eyes. The tears dried, replaced with abject terror.

"I don' know who spilled on Heihachi, but you won' say another word to anyone about it," Enoch said. "You're gettin' thrown to the wolf."

"No, please!"

"They did a real clean job on him." Enoch rose from his chair and walked to the door. "I bet a thousand gil you thought he was flatlined."

Shock overtook fear for a brief moment.

"He's . . . not?"

"You can't kill my *kazo*," Enoch said. "But you gotta pay the price for trying."

"Key . . .?"

Enoch shook his head.

"Worse."

Enoch swung the door wide. Six stood on the threshold. She walked into Enoch's office, rage pouring off her like a physical force. Chibi expected her to shoot Nat, maybe just beat the shit out of her, but Six's hate was far more controlled than her husband's. If he was a blazing fire, she was a blowtorch — focused.

"Listen, Six, I —"

Six didn't even need to speak. The mere look in her eye was enough to make Nat fall silent.

"I'm sorry," Nat wept. "They told me Key was secretly a monster . . . they said all sorts of things about what he did before . . ."

"And you believed them."

It wasn't a question. It was an accusation. Six pulled out a small, silver object — a scalpel.

"Let me tell you what's going to happen, okay?" Six said flatly. "I am going to cleanly sever your femoral artery."

She paused, waiting for the fear and anticipation to take hold.

"While you are bleeding out, I will apply pressure so you don't die too quickly."

She took the rubber guard off the blade.

"Do you know why?"

Nat shook her head slowly, the dread incrementally forcing her out of her body.

"Because I want you to tell me who you spoke with," Six said. "I want to know who set this whole thing up in the first place."

Nat was frozen. If Six was waiting for something, she wasn't going to get it.

"Think you can manage that?"

Six moved without the answer, slicing into Nat's leg with skill and precision. Nat didn't even scream in pain. That is until Six applied the pressure.

"AAAAAGH!!" Nat wailed.

"I lied," Six said, grabbing Nat by the back of the neck and drawing her close. "I don't care if you tell me who put you up to this."

Six used the scalpel to cut Nat's cheek.

"They shot him four times . . ." Six whispered, cutting Nat's other cheek. "Set him on fire."

"Please, Six . . ." Nat moaned, already starting to slip a bit. "He's not who you think . . ."

Six stepped back, releasing Nat's leg.

"I want you to die," Six said, ignoring Nat's own accusations. "I want you to feel the fear of your life falling through your fingers."

The color started to drain from Nat's face as her pupils dilated. Beads of sweat formed on her forehead.

"I . . . I was . . ." she murmured.

The blood pooled in the chair and spilled onto the floor.

"I wanted . . ."

Her eyes fluttered as she lost consciousness. Six jammed the scalpel into Nat's forehead.

Key sat at the bar, the nightlife raging around him. He still couldn't decide what the hell he was going to do. He knew he was going to do *something,* but he couldn't figure out what it was. He could blow up Zaibatsu, but that hardly seemed productive. He could dig himself a hole, set up some traps, and wait for the headhunters to come for him, shooting out like an antlion when they did. Whatever the solution, his chances of catching bullets were high.

I can take a bullet . . . he thought. *Or twenty.*

It didn't seem likely he'd be able to win regardless of what he did; he was a small man who had provoked a very large beast.

"Hey, *kazo!*" Enoch said, talking over the music as he approached the bar.

Key turned, finishing off his drink. Enoch leaned over, his cheek touching Key's as he spoke into his ear. Key could smell blood.

"One traitor flat," Enoch said. "Just gotta clean the other."

"Think he knows we're coming?"

"There's no way he doesn't."

CHAPTER 30
ABSOLUTE DARK

It was decided that Gode would wait until morning. He never left his little gopher hole, so he wasn't going anywhere. Unfortunately, that wasn't sitting well with Key.

He knows we're coming. Key thought, *Every second is more time for him to get ready . . . more time for Kigen to close in, too.*

He lay in bed staring at the ceiling, trying desperately to sleep. He had never taken particular note of his ceiling, but that flash — that fragment of a memory he had — wrapped in a white ceiling had caught his attention. Then again, that wasn't the only time the past had overtaken the present. He'd thought about it often since then, trying to replicate the effect. He'd hoped to spark other memories in the same manner, but he had no luck. He'd come to believe that maybe it had just been the lingering effects of the Red Room on his mind. Still, that night he searched for the trigger. He needed answers and direction; he hoped that a fragment — any solitary piece of his past — would help him face the people that hunted him. There was no better consultant than himself. If only he could remember.

Maybe I wasn't that smart to begin with, he thought. *I was a Kigen scientist or something . . . that seems like something I'd want to forget.*

Blood like acid, skin like fire.

Fuck.

He could feel it. It was faint, but it still covered his skin in discomfort. Ever since he'd unlocked those fragments of his past, he'd been unable to remember without the sensation forcing him to back off. He decided to tough it out this time.

Remember.

He tried to think about his mother — one of the most powerful fragments of the past he'd uncovered. All he had was a saying, a proverb, but he hoped it would spark further memories.

Hiding the garbage doesn't get rid of the smell.

He tried to remember her voice as she said it. The face she made when she no doubt scolded him with those words. He couldn't find anything.

Fuck!

He angrily got out of bed, striding into the living room. There, still with no home of his own, Chibi slept. At least they'd been able to get a futon so he had an actual place to sleep. Key grabbed his jacket and stormed out the door. He paused just outside, half turning back as he reconsidered what he was about to do. He clenched both fist and jaw, making up his mind.

"Jarvis."

"Yes, sir?" the AI replied.

"Execute Absolute Dark grid protocol, auth code 03172019."

"Confirming complete shutdown of all external signals. Apartment will be cut off from electrical and communications with triple-wall door reinforcement. In the case of forced entry, you have authorized the use of force. This AI unit will be authorized to commit murder. The authorizing individual will be held legally responsible for any repercussions of —"

"Confirmed," Key interrupted.

"Set unlock key?"

Key was about to lock his wife and friends in his apartment

with no way to leave or contact the outside world. He hesitated a moment.

I have to keep them safe. Who knows who's coming after me?

"Set key to Final Answer."

"Key accepted," Jarvis said. "Beginning Absolute Dark Protocol in 5 . . . 4 . . . 3 . . ."

Key looked back through the open door. Against the far wall, Ajax sat staring. Key knew he had seen. Knew he'd heard. Ajax was fully aware he was about to do something stupid. Yet, for all he knew, the Oran watched the doors close. Ajax didn't stop him.

In the Underground again, Key paddled his way towards the troll. This would be a quick meeting. Key had no faith that the goblin man would share any intel, so he wasn't going to bother. A simple eye for an eye. This time, he wasn't going to be caught off guard.

"Halt!"

Nekros approached the raft, always the arbiter of the canal.

"Ababheki. Ere di ohia —"

"You speak the words, but I know you not!"

"It's Key, Nekros!"

"Key . . .?" Nekros muttered. "Key . . ."

Key decided to just keep paddling.

"The devils are coming for you, friend," Nekros called to him. "I have seen it in the wisps."

This caught Key's attention. He stopped paddling, turning in his raft.

"Who's coming for me?"

Nekros may have been a bit out of touch with reality, but few people were more aware of the buzz on the web. The only difficulty was getting the info out of him.

"Myriad fiends," Nakros answered. "I know some by name."

"Kigen sent them?"

"Indeed. Or rather, they will," Nekros replied. "The dragon is full of wrath and is sending many foul beasts to retrieve you."

Retrieve . . .?

"The devils aren't trying to kill me?"

"I should think not," Nekros said. "You are very important to the great dragon. It certainly does not want you harmed."

"But Med-Sec does."

"Quite," Nekros agreed. "One has placed a price on your head, the other wishes you unharmed. Who shall prevail in their quest?"

Key took up the paddle. "We'll see, won't we?"

As the raft glided past Nekros, the self-appointed gatekeeper held out his gaunt hand. Slightly confused but very intrigued, Key took his hand. He looked into Nekros's eyes. There was a clarity to them that one rarely saw.

"Be safe, Key."

KEY PADDLED past the still knocked-over floodlights from his fight with Tengu's boys. Their bodies were gone. He paddled past the stations with their varied décor. Some maintained and some fallen to ruin, each was a relic of a different time, but life moved on. He paddled to the terminal with its dark beauty. The waterfall and the greenery swallowing the remnants of industry. He docked.

No time to waste.

Disembarking from his vessel, Key walked down the hall. He could hear the echo of the sniper shot that took him down the last time. He looked around, checking the offices for any hidden assailants. Unfortunately, he was right.

Damn.

He spotted them out of the corner of his eye. As he opened a door to check one of the offices, someone burst from the one to his left. He had no time to evade or counter, only raise his arm and hope the bullet didn't go through.

BAM!

A shotgun blast. Key wasn't expecting that. He took a lot of the pellets to his arm, but some caught him in the chest. It chewed his arm's plating to shreds.

BANG! BANG! BANG!

His shot was blind, but he got a decent enough look at where the shooter was and felt good about at least one of those shots. Not one to rest on his laurels, he dove into the office he'd just opened.

BAM!

The shot blasted into the wall, throwing tile shards into the hall and peppering Key in dust. He reached around the corner to loose a couple more shots.

BANG! BANG!

BAM!

He'd gotten the timing. They must have been using a pretty slow loader, but it paid off in damage. Key was lucky he took the shot to his off hand.

BAM!

That was his moment. He popped out of the office, low to the floor and quick as a jackrabbit as he popped two shots.

BANG! BANG!

The other guy's head snapped back and he fell to the floor, the shotgun slipping from his hand. Key took a breath, surveying the area to make sure the guy didn't have any backup. Coast was clear.

Damn.

Key stood over the dead guy. Blood ran from the guy's leg and forehead.

Two hits. he thought. *Not bad.*

Key knew it was too easy. There was no way that was one of the mercs Katsuwara would have sent. Granted, if Nekros was to be trusted, those guys wouldn't be trying to blow off his head anyway.

More to come.

He elected not to dwell on it. He had something he needed to do. He did a quick frisk of the corpse to see if he had anything good on him. Nothing. Key tugged at his ear; it still echoed with a dull ringing from the firefight. He knew a guy who got his hearing replaced with bionics that could sense loud noise and shut off. Maybe he'd look into that after this mess was settled.

I certainly shoot enough bullets.

Key walked to the end of the hall, kicking in the office door. Gode sat behind his desk, death-gripping a pistol that was way too high-caliber for him to handle.

"Don' youse take anotha step!" Gode shouted, his obvious terror undercutting any threat.

"What are you gonna do?" Key asked. "Shoot me?"

BOOM!

The recoil knocked the gun out of Gode's hand, the bullet way off its mark.

"You're fucking pathetic," Key spat.

He didn't bother with a monologue or insults. One shot was all this shit-smear deserved.

The first of many to come.

BANG!

ABOUT THE AUTHOR

Ryan McKinney always knew he wanted to be a writer. He wrote his first book, *Finbur and the Lily,* on dot-matrix printer paper at the age of six. Today he writes books about technology, the future, and the human condition.

Before finishing his debut novel, *Neon Nothing,* Ryan earned an undergraduate degree in English literature and American history, and a master's degree in cybersecurity policy.

An East Coast native, Ryan McKinney lived in New York, Maryland, and Virginia, before finally settling down in Greenville, North Carolina. When he's not pouring himself into his writing, Ryan is a professional tutor and supplemental instructor for his local community college.

Find out more about Ryan, including news about forthcoming books, at www.ryanmckbooks.com.

www.ingramcontent.com/pod-product-compliance
Lightning Source LLC
Chambersburg PA
CBHW020558310726
48979CB00008B/1259/J